THE GIRL ON THE SWING
and
AT NIGHT IN CRUMBLING VOICES

Other Books by Peter Grandbois

The Gravedigger
The Arsenic Lobster: A Hybrid Memoir
Nahoonkara
Domestic Disturbances

WORDCRAFT SERIES OF FABULIST NOVELLAS

Double Monster Features

Wait Your Turn/The Stability of Large Systems
The Glob Who Girdled Granville/The Secret Lives of Actors

NUMBER
3 WORDCRAFT SERIES OF FABULIST NOVELLAS

PETER GRANDBOIS

A DOUBLE MONSTER FEATURE

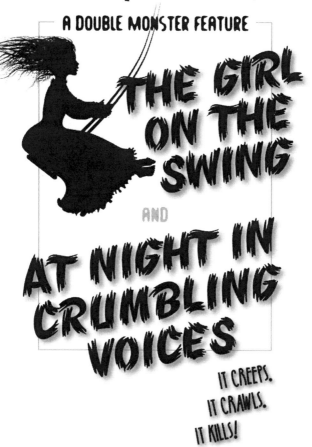

THE GIRL ON THE SWING

AND

AT NIGHT IN CRUMBLING VOICES

IT CREEPS.
IT CRAWLS.
IT KILLS!

La Grande, OR • 2015

Acknowledgments

Once again, thanks to Mike Croley, Jane Delury, and Margot Singer. The best readers ever.

Thanks, also, to David Memmott for his vision and commitment to all things monstrous.

Finally, thank you to my wife, Tanya, for putting up with the monster in me.

The Girl on the Swing was inspired by the film *The Quatermass Experiment* (Hammer Productions, 1953). *At Night in Crumbling Voices* was inspired by the film *The Mole People* (William Alland, 1956).

Copyright © 2014, Peter Grandbois
ISBN: 978-1-877655-86-9
Library of Congress Number: 2014955736
Number Three in the Wordcraft Series of Fabulist Novellas

First Edition
March 2015

Cover Design: Kristin Summers, www.redbatdesign.com
Cover graphics © DepositPhotos.com (Ola-Ola & Naddya)
Author photo: Gary Isaacs

Published by
Wordcraft of Oregon, LLC
PO Box 3235
La Grande, OR 97850
http://www.wordcraftoforegon.com
info@wordcraftoforegon.com

Member of Council of Literary Magazines & Presses (CLMP)

Text set in Garamond Premier Pro
Printed in United States

For Elena, Olivia, and Santi

THE GIRL ON THE SWING

Human nature, essentially changeable, unstable as the dust, can endure no restraint; if it binds itself it soon begins to tear madly at its bonds, until it rends everything asunder, the wall, the bonds, and its very self.

—Kafka

Before she grew everywhere she searched for her wings. She never looked at the ground then. She rarely looked at her family either. They'd call to her but it was as if she wasn't there. In her white dress and mantle she sat on the swing under the oak in the front yard. She stretched a wing toward the sky. And she woke, smiling. Then everything went empty. The world drained from her face. She didn't need it anymore. Only to swing higher and higher, to be born again each day. Her younger brother didn't understand. He grew frustrated and stopped asking her to play.

Each night her father would stand on the front porch and call her to dinner. She'd keep swinging, as if she couldn't hear. At first, he'd march down the porch steps and stand by the tree as she swung back and forth, back and forth. He'd glare at her, expecting her to notice. She wouldn't. Occasionally, he'd sneak up behind her and poke her in the back, as if to scare her off the swing. It didn't work.

At some point, he gave up trying. Come dinner time, he'd stand on the porch, the sun painting the sky with the pink haze of evening, and he'd simply watch. That's when he noticed the way in which she turned her face to the heavens and smiled with each upward arc. Martyred violets could bloom from that smile. Roses and black dahlias could fall like tears from that smile. She seemed to be talking, and he wondered what she told the clouds, what secrets she revealed.

Once, he stood below her and tried to listen, but her voice whispered past like the wind. He tried to grab her, to ask what she was saying, find out to whom she was speaking. But a bird cried, and the branch from which she swung groaned. So, instead, he lay face up on the ground and watched her from below. Clouds crowned her head. Stars garlanded her neck. He hadn't known his daughter was so beautiful. Of course, he'd known she was pretty, in the way all fathers think their daughters pretty. But to see your daughter's hair sway like leafed branches, to watch the dark center of her smile flower. That's different. That's when a father knows the kind of beauty that will hurt him in the end, hurt him in ways he never imagined. He thought he understood. He lay on the ground and told himself that he knew what was coming. But he was wrong. He knew nothing of loss, the way it can deprive you even of memory, not simply of what your child looked like, but of who she was and what you were to each other. He thought he could prepare for such a thing.

You can't.

He thought it would come in the form of a boy who would snatch her away.

It didn't.

He thought that he and his wife would be strong enough.

They weren't.

Nobody understands the many paths loss takes. No one can prepare for them all.

The next evening before dinner he watched as she

pumped the swing harder and harder, pushing until the rope curved slack at its apex and for a moment she floated weightless. She's swinging too high, he thought. The branch will break, and she'll fall to the ground, or the rope will break, and she'll career off into space. He shouted for her to slow down, to reign in her legs, to stop pumping. But she went right on talking to the clouds. He reached out for her, as if he could do anything to stop her, as if even if he could reach her and had the will to stop the swing and the strength to pull her down, he could keep from happening what then happened.

She stopped talking. She tilted her head to the side to listen. She pumped harder, pushing herself higher until he lost sight of her for a moment. Her outline against the sky. He didn't know if it was the play of light on the leaves or if perhaps she simply disappeared behind some branches, or if a cloud settled about her, obscuring her from view. He would have believed any of these possibilities instead of what seemed to have happened, what he knew had to have happened.

When she returned, she was smiling. He wondered why he used the word "returned" when he thought about it after. But what other explanation could there be for the events that followed? She had to have traveled someplace else. How else could he account for the shift in her smile when he caught sight of her again? A smile like leaves around her twitching mouth. She kept swinging as if to the sound of a faint drum, some rhythm he couldn't hear. The scent of clover filled the air. She arced her neck and took in a deep breath, as if it would be her last. She turned to him with eyes like an empty field, and he could see for miles. She didn't look at him at all.

She stopped swinging, walked passed him, went inside, sat down at the kitchen table and quietly ate an apple. She ate everything, the core, the seeds, the stem. When she was done, she grabbed the entire bag of apples and ate them one by one as she stood at the counter. Her brother complained that he wouldn't have one for lunch the next day. Her mother commented that her daughter should be careful not to spoil her appetite as she'd cooked her favorite meal. But their complaints breezed through her ears. After dinner, she went straight to bed, which was unusual. Her father was accustomed to her reading for hours before bedtime, and, of course, the inevitable fights about homework.

When he went to tuck her in, he found her lying in the middle of the bed, completely still, her hands open and raised above her as if trying to catch something. She didn't move. She didn't blink. He pulled the covers about her and sat down beside her.

"Are you okay?" he asked. "You seem distant tonight."

For a moment she remained frozen, and for no particular reason he could think of later, he started to panic. Then she tilted her head toward him, her eyes narrowing as if trying to see. "How do I know you're my daddy?" she asked.

He smiled and patted her head. His daughter was playing a joke at his expense, he thought. He could play along. "You don't," he replied. "You're probably the milkman's daughter." The ceiling fan rattled above them. When had it gone out of alignment?

"You're not my daddy," she said.

Twelve year olds can have a strange sense of humor. He waited for her to laugh, to crack a smile. Nothing.

The air quivered between them. A branch scratched at her window. He kissed her on the forehead, studying her eyes as he pulled away. "You're my daughter. I know that much." He ran his fingers through her hair. She flinched as if he'd hit her.

"I thought you liked a good head scratch," he said, forcing his own smile now.

"Not tonight." She rolled away, giving her back to him.

"Did I do . . .?"

The unspoken words hovered like a fly over the bed.

The next morning she had trouble getting dressed. When he asked her why, she said she didn't know what to wear. He knocked on her door, and she yelled at him to leave her alone. When he eventually threatened she'd miss school, she emerged wearing a loose fitting sweatshirt, a green scarf wrapped about her left hand.

"Isn't it a bit warm for that?" He offered her a plate of honey toast.

She walked passed him, sitting on the couch away from her brother who sat finishing his cereal at the kitchen table. Their mother was already at work.

"Yeah, it's like a hundred degrees out," her brother offered between bites. "You're going to sweat like crazy."

"It's different where I'm at." She reached her scarfed hand toward a potted white orchid on the end table next to her.

Her father stepped forward as if to stop her, though he was unsure why.

Her brother rolled his eyes. "Where's that? The land of the stupid sisters?"

She pulled her hand away, scratching under the scarf.

"Do we have any fruit?" she asked. "A banana would be nice."

"Sure, sweetie," her father replied. "But you better eat it in the car. We're late for school."

She stood to go, but almost as soon as she did, she started to sit back down again, her hand reaching for the orchid.

"Are you okay?" her father asked, her brother flying past them both, grabbing the loose and crumpled sheets of homework that always seemed to be scattered on the floor and stuffing them in his backpack.

"I'm fine," she said, her gaze fixed on the orchid. She took a deep breath, grabbed her backpack, and walked to the door.

Three hours later, her father received a call from the school nurse asking if he could pick her up. She'd grabbed a cactus in the science room and had gotten a few thorns lodged in her hand. Not normally enough to send her home, the nurse admitted, but the thorns penetrated particularly deeply, and she was worried about infection.

On the car ride home, his daughter seemed unwilling to talk, gazing out the back window at the oak and sycamore that seemed so prevalent around town.

"Does it hurt?" he asked, unable to bear the silence.

"No."

"But it must."

"It doesn't hurt me. This is not me."

"Who is it, then?" He could play along, he thought. She'd always had an active imagination. He'd encouraged it. He wasn't going to back away now.

"I don't know."

He looked in the rear view mirror, trying to get her

attention, to force her to meet his gaze. She wouldn't, so he pulled over, got out and entered the rear of the car. She backed against the side door, staring at him, as if he were a stranger. "Can I see it?" he asked. "Your hand, I mean."

She offered her arm and let him unwrap the scarf, then peel away the bandages the nurse had placed on the wound. Dark bruises laced the area where the thorns had entered. Angry pus oozed from the holes. "Did the nurse disinfect this?" he asked.

"She put some stuff on it."

"Jesus, I hope so." He pulled out his handkerchief and rubbed away the pus. Something protruded from the back of her left hand. A sharp bump just under the skin. "I don't think she got all the thorns out," he said.

She pulled her hand away and wrapped it again with the scarf.

"Hey! Let me see that," he said. "I might be able to get it out."

"Can I walk home?" she asked. "It's only about a mile." She looked at him as if daring him to say no.

"Of course," he replied. "You can do whatever you want." But she'd already opened the door.

"I can't go back," she whispered to herself as she stepped free of the car.

Two days later, a Saturday morning, and he and his wife emerged from their bedroom to find their children playing *Legos* on the floor. Isabel looked more pale than usual. Dark circles lined her eyes. Her hair thatched into a nest. She'd slept in the same clothes she'd worn the day before. But still, both children were smiling as they worked to build a vast cityscape full of bridges and towers.

"I like what you're doing," the mother said. "Very creative." She gave her husband a look that suggested he worried too much.

"When we're done," the brother said. "I'm going to blow it all up, and Isabel said she'd help me!" His face glowed as it always did when he had someone to play with.

"Last night, they came," Isabel said, as her brother put the finishing touches on their tallest tower. "I didn't call them, but they came."

Her father reached for her scarfed hand, but she pulled it away.

"Who came?" the mother asked.

"The people I live with now." She stared at both parents with unblinking eyes.

Her brother looked up from his tower, clearly irritated. "Let's play!"

Her father took a step closer to her, worry clawing at his chest. "Isabel," he whispered, as if he didn't want her brother to hear. "You live with us."

"Do we have more fruit?" she asked, standing now and moving to the couch. "I need more fruit."

"I knew it," the brother cried. "Just when we were having fun! Now no one will play with me."

The mother smiled and sat next to her son. "I'll help you blow it all up," she said, then knocked over one of the towers with her hand.

"Not yet!" the brother cried. "I'm not ready."

The father studied his daughter once again, trying to figure out if she was pulling his leg.

"More fruit," she repeated, turning her gaze to the orchid.

He tried to get his wife's attention, but she was either too absorbed in giving to their son or unwilling to see what was happening with their daughter.

"More fruit!" She caressed the petals of the orchid.

He brought her a banana, and she smiled as she ate it.

In seconds, her brother and mother destroyed the *Lego* city. After, her mother made herself a coffee while her brother took advantage of the moment to describe to his sister the video game he wanted for Christmas. She sweated profusely as she listened to him, as if it were an exertion for her to be near them.

"Where are you?" her father asked, sitting beside her.

She rapped the back of her scarfed hand with the knuckles of her right, as one would knock on a door.

"Isabel, you don't seem present," the mother said as she sat on the ottoman opposite their daughter.

"You're not present much." Isabel knocked harder around the thorn on the back of her hand.

"I work."

"You're always at work." Her brother plopped himself in her mother's lap.

"It's not easy starting a new career in your forties," she replied.

"I work, too," the father said. "Doesn't anyone understand that?"

"You teach two classes a semester," his wife replied. "That's not work."

Isabel hit the back of her hand particularly hard.

"Stop that!" Her father grabbed her right hand, held it even as she kept trying to hit her other hand with it.

She looked at him, and he thought she might hurt him. She tried to hit herself again, but he held firm. "I'm not going to let you do that," he said. She turned her left hand over and banged it against the back of the table. "What are you doing?" he shouted, trying to grab that hand as well.

"I need to loosen things up for it to grow," was all she said.

After, he and his wife slipped back into their bedroom and closed the door.

"You're giving her the attention she wants," his wife said, turning on him.

"Are you nuts? She was hitting herself for Christ's sake!" He sat down at the small desk they kept in their bedroom for his wife to work and turned on the computer. There must be something on the web he could find out about this. "Why would she hit herself?"

"I told you." His wife approached him, took his hands in her own. "She wants attention. And the more you give it to her, the more she'll see that it works."

He sat and turned to the computer, googled "pale skin." "Did you see the way she looked, her hair?"

"Yes, I saw it." She closed the screen on their laptop and squeezed in next to him on the chair. "She's going through changes and that can be scary. You need to be strong for her, and for me."

Case Study: Isabel

Quantitative Trait Loci studies suggest that many fundamental traits are controlled by numerous small-effect loci, indicating these traits may be resistant to metamorphosis. For example, subject's obsession with reading seems to have carried over past mitosis of the apical meristem. From conversations with the parents, we have determined that prior to accelerated mitosis, subject exhibited an IQ in the gifted range combined with higher than normal physical dexterity, evident in the fact that subject competed quite successfully in fencing and badminton. Further, subject enjoyed music, playing several instruments, most notably the flute. Note: it became clear sometime in Prometaphase that the subject would no longer be able to play the flute, causing the subject distress. Subject's social life shows less distinction in that the subject tended to keep one friend at a time, though that friend was very close. Sadly, the ability to maintain this friendship was also lost as the subject entered Metaphase. Most damaging, however, was the loss of subject's relationship with her sibling (brother) during the late Anaphase when the kinetochores suddenly separated.

All indicators point to the fact that in early Prophase the subject showed normal (with the exception of her high intelligence score) development. Her parents report that she was generally happy, particularly enjoying those times when the family played games together. Her favorites included: spoons, *Uno, Clue,* and *Dungeons and Dragons*. She seemed to dislike *Monopoly* because of its capitalist overtones (once again pointing to her unusually high IQ). Initial experiments reveal no indication in early Prophase of the accelerated mitosis and mutant growth phase that followed. One test seemed to indicate an excess of protease, which could lead to cohesion breakdown, but it's far too early to make any definitive statements. In fact, it's important to state at this early stage that nothing is certain. All we know, to quote the child's father, is that, "One day she was out swinging in the front yard, reaching for the sun. The next, her legs were sending tendrils into the ground beneath her bed."

Isabel spent the evening on the swing. She held on with only her right hand, reaching her left out toward the oak, letting the scarf trail behind it. Her mother and father watched from the front porch, unwilling to move closer for fear they might startle her and she'd lose her tenuous grip.

"The tree is calling me," she said to no one in particular. "It's trying to tell me something."

He'd learned already it was sometimes better not to engage these flights of fancy, but her mother hadn't seen enough. She still operated under the assumption that this was her daughter, while he was no longer sure.

"Where does it speak?" her mother asked, stepping down from the porch, thinking it was possible to approach her. "Where is its mouth?"

"You see that split at the top where the trunk turns gray?" Isabel pointed high up the tree with her scarfed hand.

"Yes," her mother replied, as if she could actually see it. "Yes, I do!"

"And there, the mushrooms growing out around it?" his daughter continued. "The mushrooms are the beard that lines the mouth."

For some reason her father didn't fully understand, he thought it good to end their conversation. He approached his wife. "Dear . . ." he said, but it was too late. The words were already out of her mouth.

"What's it saying?" her mother asked.

"Never mind," he said. "It's late. We should go to bed." He took his wife by the hand and tried to pull her back inside, but she shot him an angry look and pulled her hand away.

"Hey!" he shouted a bit too loud, trying to shoo her inside. "You don't want to hear this."

"Don't tell me what I want to hear." Her voice shifted to a deeper register, one that signaled they were entering familiar terrain. She felt he controlled too much of her relationship with the children because he spent more time with them. He felt she didn't understand them because she was consumed with her work. Neither were right. Both of them were right. These arguments were never resolved. They simply went on and on, rising and falling, like a Ferris wheel.

She forced a smile and turned back to their daughter. "What's it saying?" she repeated.

Just as he knew he shouldn't fight, he knew in this moment he shouldn't listen. He should walk away, he thought. Let his wife hear, if she had to. She could handle it better than him. She'd store it away some place where it wouldn't harm her, if she heard it at all. But of course he listened. He had to listen in the same way he had a habit of needling his bruises in order to feel the pain.

"He says he ate a human last night," she shouted as if she were so high, so far away from them, she thought they might not hear. "He says that soon I will, too."

The hard silence of the wood tore at the air. Lidless leaves floated down upon them. His wife turned and went inside. He sat on the porch and held tight to the step as if at any moment the ground might slip away.

A week later, Isabel's skin seemed sallow, as if she'd been left in a dark and humid room for too long. Her father had told her she wasn't going to school. She didn't argue. He'd asked to see her hand. She pulled it close to her chest. I'm taking you to the doctor, he told her. She's going to need to see it, so you may as well show me now. She backed toward her bookcase and the potted ivy that cascaded down from the top shelf.

"Show me your hand," he repeated. "I'm worried about you."

She pressed her back against the bookcase. He took her hand, pulled it toward his face to better see, but she resisted. Slowly, he unwrapped the scarf.

"No!" She pulled her hand away again. He lunged for her, grabbing the scarf, as she hit the bookcase, knocking the ivy to the hardwood floor with a crash. She screamed with such pain he thought she broke when the pot shattered. She fell to the floor, the scarf unraveling about her. Even as she frantically tried to gather up the dirt and shove it back into the broken pot, it was easy to see the thorn growing from her hand, quite large now, and with what seemed to be buds sprouting from it.

That afternoon he called several doctors, ultimately settling on a botanist from the local university.

Soon it became difficult getting her to school. It's not that she didn't want to go. She did, at least at first. She'd pack her lunch and head to the door, but would inevitably stop in front of the ivy on the mantle or the potted palm in the entryway as if unable to move past it. She'd spend the rest of the day staring at the plant unless her father called to her. He'd tell her she'd be late for school, and she'd break away, but it was as if the plants exhibited some sort of pull on her. She wouldn't take two steps before she'd stop. You could see the struggle in her: the desire to go to school, to see her friends, to chat with her teachers and keep up her grades--in short, to continue with her normal life—all pushing against her need to be near the plants. The worst was when they'd drive past the oak as they rolled down the driveway. Several times, she tried to open the door and jump out.

Within a few weeks, her father got rid of all the plants. It didn't work. She knew where they'd been. Maybe she smelled some remnant of dirt or maybe something in her blood simply sensed trace elements of root, but she'd still stop in the same place each morning. Her father vacuumed over the spots, and when that didn't work, he vacuumed again. It became nearly impossible to get her to leave the house. He painted the passenger windows of the car black so she wouldn't be able to see the oaks, or any vegetation. But something in her knew exactly where each tree was. In fact, she knew the exact location of every plant and tree along their route to school.

What scared him most was the night she disappeared. The family sat down together to watch some TV and soon realized she was nowhere to be found. They searched the house. Nothing. They searched around the swing. Nothing. They called her friends. The neighbors. Nothing. Eventually, they scoured the forest beyond their land. It was ten o'clock on a cold October night, and none of them could have guessed that she'd taken a shovel from the garage and dug a hole for herself beside an oak at the edge of the forest. They were lucky. She'd stopped to rest and fallen asleep in the hole before she could bury herself. They found her lying in the bottom, the only clue she wasn't dead being the frozen vapor coming from her nose in short, moth-like puffs.

Somewhere near the end of the first month, she stopped covering her left hand with the scarf. It was no longer practical. The thorny tendril rising from it stood out a good six inches now. She didn't seem embarrassed by it any more. If asked to set the table by her mother, she would do so, allowing for the times she hesitated as she passed the mantel where the ivy used to sit or the end table where the orchid used to grow. Her brother gave the hand a longer than usual glance the first time he saw it without the scarf. But after that he seemed to take it in stride. On those rare occasions any more when he and his sister played together, he'd hand her a toy without flinching. But when he gave her the controller the time she sat next to him on the couch to play video games, the father pulled it from them and washed it with bleach. After, he went to the store and bought a year's supply of anti-bacterial wipes and scrubbed the whole house down. His family watched him work, unsure whether they should help or tell him to stop.

His wife didn't seem to notice their daughter's hand at all. He accused her of burying her head in the sand where the issue of their daughter was concerned.

"She's ill," he said as he locked the master bedroom door behind them. "Something has happened to her, and we need everyone in this family to be on the same page."

She stopped writing but did not set down her pen, turning toward him ever so slightly. "My head is not in the sand. I know she's suffering. I simply don't see it as being as serious as you do."

"She's got a plant growing out of her hand!" he yelled. "Her skin looks like an onion that's been left in the pantry too long. Are you listening?"

She capped her pen, set it down, then slowly began gathering and stacking her papers. He could hear the birds chirping outside their window. One bird in particular, a Black Capped Chickadee, drove him crazy with its shrill, three-part whistle. "Yes," she said. "Yes. Yes, I'm listening."

"Good," he began, "because I want to . . ."

"But that doesn't change the fact that I still think you're overreacting." She put her papers in her briefcase.

He took her by the shoulders, forcing her to look at him. "Do you know anyone whose daughter has something growing out of her hand?"

"It's a little stick," she replied. "It's not that bad. Everyone has something wrong with them. I've got eye problems and look at you and your stomach issues."

"Leave my stomach out of it!" he shouted, then realizing their children were probably hearing every word, he turned on the portable CD player on their bedside table. He sat on the bed, head in hands.

"It doesn't seem to bother her brother," his wife went on. "It doesn't seem to bother her friends." She disappeared in the closet to plan her wardrobe for the next day.

"Are you saying it's me?" He followed her into the closet. "That I'm the problem?"

"I'm saying you might be part of it. Just think about it." She handed him a pair of shoes.

"And what if it doesn't stop with her hand? What if it works its way up her arm? What if it turns her whole arm into a tree?"

"We'll cross that bridge when we get to it." She draped a blouse over his arm. "Your problem is you always think too many steps ahead. You always worry about the future."

He'd always been a worrier. And where had it

gotten him? An ulcer before the age of fifty. Migraines. A receding hair line. A bad back. He needed to let go. But that night in bed he couldn't stop thinking about her hand. It floated in the space before his eyes, the onion skin, the network of veins pulsing beneath it. The hand seemed to have hundreds more tiny veins than it could possibly need, as if what grew from it required an abnormal amount of nourishment. Strangely, the extra veins didn't help her skin. The flesh around that thorny tendril was beginning to cave in on itself. Was it his imagination or was her hand starting to stink? He was sure he could smell the rotting flesh when she passed him. The last time he looked, he could have sworn there was something like gangrene spreading from her wrist and up her arm. What if that were true? What if it started to affect the rest of her body?

He found himself standing over her bed, holding her hand, examining it as best he could in the dark. Yes, he could smell the contaminated flesh beyond her wrist. He could see the network of veins stretching now up her forearm. He was sure of it. If he pressed hard enough, he could feel the skin, muscle and bone of the lower forearm give way beneath his finger like loam.

He put his hand in his pocket, traced the outline of his Swiss Army knife. If he could just shave off some of the rotten flesh, that might do it. He wouldn't have to take off the whole hand. It would be difficult to finish before she woke up and screamed, before his wife ran into the room and pulled him from her. He almost had the knife out of his pocket before he realized what he was saying.

Case Study: The Brother

Growth rate is strongly affected by nitrogen nutrition. When plants were grown from seed, a thirty-three percent decrease in tissue nitrogen was associated with a seventy-five percent overall inhibition of leaf growth. Almost all growth inhibition resulted from depression of daytime growth rate, decreasing root hydraulic conductivity.

It has become clear fairly quickly in our analysis of the younger brother that the subject's separation from him and the increasing distance between them had a severe effect on his development. Interviews with the parents and several friends all paint a picture of a boy who, before his sister's germination, ran everywhere as if there was never enough time to do all he wanted. Neighbors report they couldn't remember seeing him without a smile on his face. Mostly, they remember him with his sister: how they chased each other on their way home from school, the many afternoons they played in the woods outside their home, Saturday mornings making chalk drawings on the driveway, most any evening the two of them riding their scooters up and down the neighborhood street.

Water content and hydraulic conductivity are strongly affected by plant water stress. In short, plant function suffers. Despite the brother's attempts to appear normal, nuclear magnetic resonance imaging reveals cracks in the internal flow hydraulics of related tissue. It is our hypothesis that these cracks are not the result of abnormalities or genetic defects, but rather represent the result of environmental factors within the home, particularly those surrounding the severed relationship with the subject. To put it bluntly, fundamental changes in the subject's morphology have resulted in the brother's decreased ability to complete normal cell-to-cell transport. The result may not reveal itself in the short term, but long-term damage is inevitable.

Her screams woke the father from his position on the floor outside her bedroom. In an instant, he switched on the light and was at her side. She reached out to him with her left hand, the hand he'd been unable to bring himself to cut off just a few hours before. The fingers had changed. If you could call them that. Instead, five slender styles spread out from her palm, each one separated into five bushy red stigma, as if her hand were some kind of flower—a putrid flower whose rot extended up her forearm and all the way to her shoulder. Several thorny sprouts shot up from the decaying flesh around her elbow and within her armpit.

The animal that lived now permanently in his chest clawed without remorse until he couldn't breathe.

"What is happening to me?" She held her arm out to him, as if she expected him to take it away, to make it better somehow. But all he could do was sit down on the bed beside her. It was his fault, he should have cut off her hand when he had the chance.

"Daddy?" She touched him with it, with the thing that was her arm.

He grabbed it, nearly lifting her from the bed as he pulled it closer to his face. With his free hand, he pulled out his pocketknife. It was not yet too late.

His daughter's eyes quickened like a cornered animal. "What are you doing?" She tried to pull her hand away, but his grip was too strong.

He managed to peel out the saw blade even as he held her. "It's for the best," he said. "I have to stop it."

She hit him with her fist, knocking the knife from his hand. "Daddy! Daddy! Daddy!" she screamed.

He let go of her arm. "What did you say?" Again, the

rattle of the ceiling fan, marking time.

She pulled her arm to her chest, protected it there. "Get out!" she shouted at him. "Get out of my room!"

His wife came running in, bleary eyed, in her robe. "What's going on?" She saw the pocketknife on the floor. She saw the terror on her daughter's face and the look of confusion on her husband's. She put two and two together. "Have you lost your mind? What kind of a monster are you?" Not questions exactly, but a way of focusing her rage as she hit him hard on the side of the head.

"Monster?" He backed away from them both. "Who are you calling a monster?"

His wife turned on him, jabbing her finger in his face. "Let's not do this here. Not in front of her."

"You're the monster," he said, swatting her hand away. "How do you not see what she's going through?"

"I see plenty, goddamn it!" she screamed. "I just deal with it differently. Is that okay with you?"

He didn't know what to say. He hadn't thought of this, hadn't thought maybe it was affecting her, too, eating her from the inside out.

"Stop it," their daughter said so quietly they almost didn't hear. "Stop doing this." It was as if her voice was receding inside her, as if it, too, was being absorbed.

They both sat down on the bed next to their daughter, the mother caressing her forehead, trying to soothe her. Their daughter flinched under the touch, pulling her head back as if the caresses hurt. At first he was angry that his wife didn't seem to notice. He almost yelled at her again, but then he saw how her other hand shook as it reached out for him. He took her hand in his own. She leaned her head toward him, whispering in his ear.

"I don't know how much more of this I can take."

"I understand." He pulled her closer to him than he had in a long time.

She stood to go, then saw the knife on the floor. She picked it up, held it between them. "We need to call someone," she said. "A doctor."

"I did."

"What kind of person calls a botanist for their daughter?" She pocketed the knife.

"He's already talked to her. Says he wants to meet with both of us, too." He fought the urge to reach out to her, to draw her closer to him once again.

She let out a breath like a thousand cicadas sucking the life from her. "I sure hope you're right," she said, looking as if there was something else to be said, only she couldn't quite remember what it was. "Good night." She left the room. He was grateful she didn't say more.

He turned to his daughter who pulled the covers up to her neck. "You did say, "Daddy," didn't you?"

She regarded him with distant eyes. "You weren't there," she said.

"You still called me Daddy." He adjusted the covers about her. "I heard it. When you were scared, you called me Daddy."

"You weren't there when I called," she replied. "You were somewhere else."

He turned out the light and lay down on the floor in the far corner of the room. His right hand hurt where he'd grabbed his daughter. In the dark, he ran his thumb over his palm only to find a thorn pricked deep into the flesh beneath his ring finger. He pulled it out and sucked away the spot of blood. He sat for a long while, staring into the darkness above her bed, listening to the hours of predawn rain like a beating.

The next morning, she came to breakfast doused in her mother's perfume.

"Good idea," he said as he carried the milk to the kitchen table for her. "It will hide the smell." Her left arm hung useless now. She carried two bananas to the table with her right.

Her brother descended the stairs from his room, rubbing the sleep from his eyes. His hair stuck up from his head. He grabbed a bowl of cereal and sat on the opposite end of the table from his sister.

"Isn't the side chair your usual?" her father asked.

The brother simply shrugged. "I felt like something different," he said, arranging the cereal boxes around him like a castle wall, closing him off from the rest of the family.

Her father sat down between them, trying to make conversation as he ate his honey toast. "Have your friends said anything?" he asked. When she didn't respond, he followed with "And what about your music teacher? What does she say when you can't play the flute?"

She looked at him as if he were a fly buzzing about her face, an irritant she couldn't be rid of. "They don't notice," she said, rising to return to her bedroom.

"What are you talking about?" He stood to follow. "Surely someone must have said something. It's getting a little obvious."

She stopped at the stairs going down to her room. "You don't understand. It doesn't seem to bother them."

"Why?" He had so many questions, and he didn't

like the fact that once she got to her room, she tended to stay there. He had to keep her from going. "Don't they see that you're not happy about it? Don't they care that it stops you from doing things? Being normal?"

"I am normal," she replied, descending the steps. "Just not the same normal as I used to be."

"But it's affecting your schoolwork." He ran after her, stopping at her door, as if he were afraid to enter. "You're having trouble writing now. And I know how much you loved the flute."

"What am I supposed to do, Dad?" she asked, turning on him, grabbing the door. "Give up? Let you do everything for me? Do you want to play with my friends, too?" She closed the door between them.

Her tangled hair made it increasingly difficult to see her face, and he'd always loved her smile. He'd prided himself on his ability to get her to smile no matter what her mood. But now her hair, if you could call it that, wound like vines about her head and down about her face. He'd tell her to comb it each morning, but of course she didn't. He didn't know if she was ignoring him on purpose or if it was because she was now losing the ability to use her right hand, the fingers of that hand turning to pistils only a few days before.

He rarely slept with his wife. She'd go to bed early anyway, working until she fell asleep. He didn't understand how she slept so easily. He couldn't. At first the lack of sleep bothered him. He told himself he'd survived those early weeks on coffee alone, but the truth was he didn't want the coffee, or rather, that he preferred the somnambulant state. There was something satisfying about living one's waking life so close to that of dreaming. Nothing made sense to him anyway. At least in the dream world, he didn't expect it to.

Soon, he found he needed very little sleep at all. He stayed up reading. Books on plant anatomy and physiology at first. It seemed like a natural choice, though not being trained as a biologist, he found the books to be over his head. His attention span wasn't what it used to be, not since the changes in his daughter, not since the sleep deprivation. On those nights when the scientific language proved too much for him, he turned to shorter books. Poetry. One of the first books he picked up was a book by Robert Bly that had been given to him years ago as a present. He normally didn't read poetry. He'd always assumed the friend who gave him the book simply wanted to be rid of it. But now here he was not just reading the book, but rereading one stanza of one poem in particular:

> *The strong leaves of the box-elder tree*
> *Plunging in the wind call us to disappear*
> *Into the wilds of the universe*
> *Where we shall sit at the foot of a plant*
> *And live forever like the dust.*

Is that what had happened to his daughter that evening on the swing? Had she gone somewhere she wasn't supposed to, some place no one had ever traveled, a place not meant for humans, a place where human thought was alien and plant thought was the norm, a place where a plant thought had somehow entered her, somehow caused this transformation. His imagination was running rampant, and he knew it. It wasn't rational. How could swinging too high lead you to some alien place? Not to mention the very idea of plants thinking and thoughts invading you. That way madness lies.

He put down the book and stared out the living room window. The night pressed in on him, reminding him of the way the ocean had squashed his mask against his face the time he dove to one hundred feet in Cozumel as a college student. In the darkness, the trees waving in the wind looked like hands. *Nothing leaves this world without breaking.* A strange thought, but where did it come from? No. Not again. He wasn't going down that rabbit hole. "Nothing leaves this world without sharing," he whispered to himself as if in protest. He would fight back. He would not break. He would send those unwanted thoughts back to wherever they came from. *What if sharing is breaking?* No! His mind was playing tricks on him. That's what he got for reading poetry. He could try to go to sleep. Yes, that was it. He needed sleep. But all he could do was lie there, his legs twitching beneath the sheets, the need to scream at his wife to stop snoring rising in his throat.

He grabbed the brush from the bathroom sink and entered his daughter's room, waiting for his eyes to adjust to the deeper dark. He could see the outline of her on the bed, her tentacle like arms splayed out across the sheets. Her breathing sounded normal enough. He was happy she could sleep. There'd been nights when her sleep was restless, if she slept at all, the pains from the transformation being too much for her. He hated seeing her like that, with circles under her eyes, roaming about seemingly unable to make even the most basic decision:

Which fruit should she eat? Apples? Bananas? Should she have orange juice? How to pour it? Her hair so knotted about her face it was a wonder she could see at all.

He took her hair gently in his hand and ran his fingers through it. His daughter rolled to her side, almost as if acquiescing. He brushed her hair as he recited the stanza of the Bly poem over and over to her. *The strong leaves of the box-elder tree/ Plunging in the wind call us to disappear.* It was no use. The tangles proved too much. The brush got caught in the leaves. He tried taking a smaller section of hair in his hand, hoping if he worked it bit by bit he might be successful, but it didn't help. He plucked a leaf, thinking maybe if he could clear away some of the thick growth, he'd have a chance. She moaned but otherwise stayed soundly asleep. He plucked another and another. Soon he was tugging on the thicker vines. One. Two. Three. He ripped a particularly nasty one out.

She screamed awake, turning on the bedside light. "What are you doing?"

"I just wanted your hair to be nice," he said.

"What?" Her vine like arms waved in the air about her, as if looking for something to hook onto.

"You're such a pretty girl," he went on. "I wanted you to look pretty."

"Leave me alone." She tried to turn over but he held her back.

In the light, he saw clearly her mottled skin, the way the network of veins or vascular tissue or whatever it was now spread over her face. One of her arms wrapped around him. The other slithered around the bed post. "I just want people to see you the way I see you . . ." The vine-arm tightened about his chest. "You're scaring me," he said.

"I hate you." She stared at him with distant eyes.

"No," he said, as if by saying it he could push the words back in her mouth. It was getting increasingly difficult to breathe. "You're hurting me."

Her mother entered the room, and the vine-arm around him released, slipping back under the covers.

"Does no one understand that I get up at five thirty in the morning?" She asked, hands on hips, the low hanging robe showing her cleavage and reminding him that he couldn't remember the last time they'd had sex.

"He was yanking my hair out, Mom," his daughter said.

"I don't understand you," his wife said. She grabbed him by the hand and once again escorted him from his daughter's room.

In the living room, he stopped and pulled his hand from hers. "I know you see."

"Yes." She didn't turn around.

"I don't know what's worse," he continued "That you see and don't do anything or that I can't see what to do at all."

She walked to their bedroom, but he didn't follow. Instead, he pulled the armchair as close as he could to his daughter's room and slept there.

Case Study: The Mother

Numerous hypotheses have been proposed to explain the wide variation in the ability of parents to respond to offspring's needs. Comparative analyses have found little evidence to support many of these hypotheses, raising the question of what role parents have in offspring development at all.

In the case of the child's mother, we suggest we don't know enough yet about resource-foraging ability and its effect on the organism as a whole. By placing foraging ability in the broader context of plant traits, we believe we can substantiate a new empirically supported hypothesis to understand how the mother's seeming ability to focus almost completely on foraging ability allows her to deny the acute morphological changes occurring in her daughter. It is important at this time to expand our notion of what traits may be essential to the fitness of plant family structure, especially in light of the increasingly hostile dynamic between the mother and the father. In this regard, the mother's seeming inability to engage the profound morphology of her daughter may actually help preserve the family's healthy root structure. It is important to study the mother's behavior in concert with the father's as there is some evidence of stimulus-response patterning between them, more specifically, relational hostility centered in impulsivity/reactivity.

In conclusion, we suggest the need to examine correlations between foraging and the health of the larger system. Research should focus on what traits are crucial in placing that foraging ability within the broader context of plant fitness with particular attention to the ways in which the mother's foraging and consequent rejection of the daughter's condition may serve to neutralize the father's more erratic and, at times, irrational behavior.

After several months, the family fell into a routine. Though the routine was by no means comfortable for anyone, the idea of a set pattern to their day at least made it bearable. Evenings, the father would bring Isabel's dinner to her room, as she rarely if ever left it now. When she'd finished, he'd take the dishes away, passing through the living room where his wife worked at the kitchen table. His son played *Monopoly* by himself on the living room floor.

His son's imagination amazed him. He could play on his own for hours. He couldn't help but wonder if this behavior was something his son did naturally or if it was an adaptation to the fact that their family situation had changed so drastically in the last half year. The poor boy, he thought. His mother goes back to school and takes a new job; his sister transforms into something else, something none of us understands. He vowed to make it up to him, to spend some quality time with him after he did the dishes. But by the time he finished the dishes, he'd forgotten about his vow, sitting instead before his computer, researching plant varieties.

His daughter's legs had changed, extending out like knotted stilts that roamed about restlessly as if searching for something. He could no longer call them legs. He wasn't sure what to call them. Roots? Maybe. Branches? Probably not. Tentacles? He didn't want to think about that possibility. He spent more and more time consumed with identifying what his daughter was becoming. What was the difference between a lateral root and a tap root, between a leaf blade and a leaf petiole? He wanted to know these things. He needed to know them.

The hole in his hand where the thorn had punctured

hadn't healed properly. He studied it, pushing at the angry skin about the hole, working the pus out. Taking pleasure in the pain it caused him. He probed around the hole, looking for something. What? What was he looking for? He knew the answer even before he'd asked himself the question. He wanted a thorn to grow from his hand, too. A thorn that might sprout leaves. A thorn that would spread across his entire body. He studied the hole. Nothing grew from it, not even the slightest shoot. He was as far from understanding his daughter as ever. He wondered why he didn't treat his hand. It might be infected. All that pus didn't look good. He'd taken to wearing a glove to hide it, too. Like his daughter had done. He told himself he didn't want to scare his son, or alienate his wife more than she already was alien to him. But that wasn't the whole truth, and he knew it. Only late at night, when everyone was asleep, and he could roam the house, stopping occasionally to stare out the living room window at the trees waving to him in the darkness did the real truth percolate to the surface. In those moments, when the horror of the thought crept upon him, he shoved it back down to that place deep inside, and he locked the door, swearing he would not think that thought again. But of course, he did.

Then one night, the sounds coming from his daughter's room changed. They began as a banging, as if she were picking up her desk chair and slamming it on the floor over and over. The first few times it happened, he stood in the doorway of her room and watched as her tentacle arms pulled pictures from walls, books off shelves and threw them to the floor. He assumed she did this out of frustration, out of the pain of not being able to stop the changes going on inside her. He tried asking her, but when she was in these fits, she didn't answer. Or couldn't answer. When she moved on to heavier objects, he stayed away from the room. "She's exercising her new muscles, testing her strength," he told his wife as she looked up from her computer at the kitchen table. Her son didn't look up from his playing, the only sign he was aware of the sounds at all evident in the way he stopped and recounted his steps on the *Monopoly* board.

Within a week the pounding and slamming turned into an unbearable digging. Like a jackhammer in slow motion. On the first night of the digging, the son actually asked the father if he'd play *Monopoly* with him, but the father didn't hear. The son tried again, waited what must have been a good five minutes for an answer, but the louder the sounds the more intensely the father surfed the Internet. Finally, the son folded up his *Monopoly* game and went to his own room, crawled under his bed and covered his ears. Still, the father kept working. It wasn't so much that his need to find out what was happening to his daughter increased as the intensity and strangeness of the sounds from her room increased, but rather that it distracted him from the fear gnawing inside and from the thought that kept creeping up his throat from somewhere deep within.

His daughter called out to him, "Daddy, can you come here?" and he hesitated. Normally, he'd be at her door in an instant. But this time, he waited. "Daddy," she called again. He never thought it would come to this, that he wouldn't respond when she called out. He looked to his wife out of the corner of his eye with the faint hope that if he seemed immersed in something, if he hesitated, perhaps she would go in his place. But no such luck. As soon as it became clear by the nature of the pounding, drilling, and hammering that their daughter had dug through the floorboards and concrete on which their home rested and hit the rich dirt she so desired, his wife looked up with a raised eyebrow from her computer. "Well?" she said.

"If I go in, I'll only make it worse," he said. "I'll agitate her, and who knows what she'll do."

His wife folded her laptop closed and leaned over it. "If you don't go in, we'll have no idea what's going on in there. She could be digging to China for all we know." Of course by "we" she meant him. He knew it. She'd already opened her laptop and returned to her work.

As he walked down the steps to his daughter's room, the floor trembled beneath his feet. He held the railing as he called to her. "Isabel, I'm here. How can I help?" No answer. He wasn't sure if she could hear him any more, as her face already had so many more layers of tissue surrounding it. Xlyem. Phloem. Parenchyma. Sclerenchyma. Vascular Tissue. Ground Tissue. He wasn't sure what it was. She didn't seem to match anything in the plant anatomy books. All he knew was that he could still see her eyes, set back as they were in all that pulpy flesh. He wished he didn't have to see them any more. The thought surprised him as he stood before her door, hesitating to push it open. The fact that he no longer wanted to see the last vestige of what made his daughter human. That's not true. Can't be true, he thought. He loved her. More than anything, he loved her. He would do anything for her, sacrifice anything. He would die for her. He told himself he avoided her gaze because it reminded him of the daughter she used to be, the daughter she was no longer. But he knew that was a lie. He simply didn't understand the truth until he opened the door and approached his daughter, her arms and legs stretching over the bed and down into the floor, rooting deeply into the earth, new stems shooting out of her belly and chest, leafed branches sprouting from them, some sort of swollen red fruit growing from the highest of these branches, and vines hanging from some of the branches, waving about in the room as if blown by an unseen breeze. He searched for the eyes that stared back at him from deep within the layers of tissue and bark. When he found them, he wished he hadn't. For though his daughter still called him Daddy when she wanted him, though she still asked him to water her or to bring her a book to read to pass the time, she no longer seemed to see him, even when he stood before her. He didn't know if it was because he had ceased to exist in some fundamental way for her or if it was because she had moved to a different place, a place so far away she no longer saw anything clearly.

After that night, he stopped entering her room. Instead, he spent his nights in his reclining chair just outside her bedroom. He got little sleep, of course, as the digging and hammering sounds only increased. He didn't care. He had to keep guard, though from what he wasn't sure.

Since she could no longer leave her room, he took a leave of absence from his own job and began attending classes for his daughter. It wasn't as easy as he thought. First, came the problem of toting a backpack from class to class that must have weighed seventy-five pounds. The other kids didn't seem to be slowed down by their packs, but he found himself panting by the time he got to the classroom door, and if there were any stairs involved he would almost assuredly be given a tardy. The problems didn't end there. Getting the combination lock to work. Trying to get the right books in and out of the overstuffed locker. It was a nightmare, though one he willingly did for his daughter. Evenings he spent doing homework. Math was the worst. He could get through everything but that. At one point, he called out for his son, hoping maybe he could help, but when his son never responded, he was too engrossed in a word problem involving how many brownies Mary and Sue sold at fifty cents a piece before their friend Ted changed the price, to notice. He knew his wife wouldn't be of help, so once out of desperation he knocked on the door to his daughter's room, hoping perhaps they could work on the problem together. It was not a good idea. Something slammed against the door. Then again and again, each time harder than the time before, as if being pummeled by several fists, each larger than the last. "Leave me alone!" his daughter's voice shouted, and that's exactly what he did. He got the math problem wrong. But it was no surprise. He got most of the problems wrong.

He rarely saw his wife any more, and when he did they didn't talk to one another. He opened his mouth to speak to her the few times they passed in the kitchen or hallway, but he found he no longer understood her language. He lacked the simple vocabulary. And he was sure, had she attempted to speak to him, the words would fall on his ears as some utterly alien tongue. Had the experience changed him so much? He walked differently. He knew that. More slowly, carefully, as if any misstep might break him. Of course, he didn't sleep much. He didn't need to eat much anymore either. It's not that he wasn't hungry, but that most food simply didn't agree with him any more. At first he thought it might have to do with the wound in his hand, but he'd given up on that hypothesis. When he looked in the mirror, he didn't recognize the face that stared back at him, the hollow eyes, the sadness that limned the mouth. In contrast, his wife didn't seem to be changing at all. To him, she looked exactly the same as the day they'd met. Of course, he knew she'd changed. They'd been married nearly twenty years. He could look at an old photo and see that she'd certainly changed over time. But when he saw her standing before him, she looked exactly the same to him, as if time didn't exist for her at all. When she talked to him, in the days when they used to talk, it was about exactly the same things that they'd talked about twenty years before.

And their son. What had happened to their son?

He'd lost track of the boy weeks ago. He couldn't remember the last time he'd seen him. He searched his son's room and found the *Monopoly* board stuffed under his bed, the pieces scattered over the floor. That's not like him, he thought. But then he wondered how he knew that, if it was even true. Was his son neat or messy? He couldn't remember. What did he look like? He tried to picture his face. He had blue eyes, right? No, they were hazel. His smile. He could never forget his son's smile. Except he had. He could no longer see it. Frantically, he ran through the house, searching for signs of his son. He found his pile of *Legos* behind the living room couch, his toothbrush with the toothpaste still on it in the bathroom, and piled on shelf after shelf, in corner after corner, he found stories and picture books his son had written. Sheets of paper stapled together with his child's scrawl across the top. He picked up one entitled *The Incredible Disappearing Man* and thumbed through it. The pictures were quite good. He hadn't realized his son had artistic talent. In the first frame, a man, he assumed to be himself, sword fought with a boy, who must be his son. The man was huge, almost a giant in proportion to the boy. But the boy smiled as he fought, as if he wouldn't be anywhere else. In the second frame, the man stood a bit farther away from the boy, and he seemed smaller of stature. Still the boy smiled as he shouted, "You are undone!" In each succeeding frame, the man appeared farther away and smaller until in the last frame the man stood only a few inches tall. The boy pinned him to the wall with his sword, saying "Now you have to stay with me!"

For the first time in weeks, he talked to his wife. She was sure their son had been playing *Monopoly* in the living room the day before. When he told her that she'd been working late the day before and hadn't been home to see him, she gave him one of her looks, saying "Why do you always have to make this about us?" Instead of answering, he continued his search. He checked the yard. His son used to love to play outside, didn't he? He'd always said he wanted a tree house, had begged his father year after year. And year after year, his father promised he would build one, but never did. There were so many trees in their yard, he'd made the excuse he couldn't decide which tree would be best. Now he stood at the base of each and every one, peering into the branches and calling for his son. Nothing. What if he'd turned into a plant, too? he wondered. What if he was out here right now, one of these trees, and he didn't even know? He ran from plant to plant like some sort of crazed butterfly, paying particular attention to the younger sprouts and saplings. He spoke to them, caressed them, feeling for any hint of a nose, a mouth, eyes, any sign they might have been human. And that's when it hit him. The boy had wandered into his sister's room, perhaps to ask her to play, or to sleep there one night because he'd been scared. He'd wandered into her room, and she'd absorbed him.

Case Study: The Father

Plants employ widely different solutions to cope with external stressors. For example, submergence tolerant rice reduce their growth and limit their consumption of energy reserves when covered by deep floodwaters, while other species accelerate elongation following flooding in order to extend their leaves above water. Given the range of widely divergent plant responses, it's not surprising to see such varied solutions in one family. Still, the idiosyncrasy of the father's response, particularly in regard to the tension between what seems on one level to be altruistic behavior and on another something more akin to the Freudian death drive, makes one wonder at the level of complexity and even cross purpose evident in so much plant and animal behavior. Darwinian evolution explains so much, and yet at times like these we come up empty.

Plants often secrete extrafloral nectar to attract animal mutualists that defend the plants against herbivores. Something of this sort may be going on here, though it's too early to tell. The way the father sits in his chair outside her bedroom at night shows many similar behavioral features to other animal mutualists. The fact that he's taken a leave of absence from his job is indicative of the kind of sacrifices mutualists generally must undergo in order to be successful. The question is does he receive anything in return? On the surface, it seems entirely possible that the father's behavior benefits only the daughter. He sacrifices time and energy that could better be utilized for foraging and reproduction. She gets her homework done. She gets fed. She gets cared for. In this sense, the relationship may not be mutualistic at all but parasitic. And yet, another possible explanation exists—that the father is, in fact, the parasite and not the other way around. It is possible under a certain light to view the father's sacrifices as selfish in that he willingly ignores the substantial morphological changes occurring in the subject. In so doing, his sacrifices actually hold no real evolutionary value for the subject in her current state. Rather, the father's sacrifices may result in any number of problems in terms of the subject's self worth and ability to function as an autonomous entity. Further, possible benefits to the father include increased feelings of self worth as he deludes himself into thinking he is doing the right thing. At this point, there is not enough information to form a hypothesis. The only thing we are sure of is that symbiosis is occurring. That said, mutualism seems unlikely. We are inclined either to follow a hypothesis of an obligate relationship where both the father and the subject are dependent on each other or one of hyperparasitism. The fact that relationships where both parties parasitize each other are rare in the natural world doesn't detour us. Mounting evidence suggests it is a real possibility here.

The hardware store was much bigger than he'd been prepared for. Aisle upon aisle of gardening instruments. Sales signaled the fact that spring was here. Now if he could only figure out what he was doing. He'd told himself he needed to pick up mulch and gardening soil, so why then was he standing in the aisle with the pruning shears? There were so many. Shears at the end of long poles that you opened and closed by pulling on a cord. Two-handed shears and shears you could fit in your pocket. Shears with curved blades and shears with straight blades. Shears guaranteed to cut through the toughest branch and micro-shears for which he couldn't imagine a possible use. In the end, he settled on a pair that fit perfectly in the palm of his hand, one with a curved blade that wasn't too big, yet was made from a titanium alloy that promised it could sever almost anything. He never did buy the mulch or the gardening soil.

The next afternoon he went to his daughter's room. She slept mostly during the day now. She would be calm. He wouldn't have to worry about new roots or tendrils impaling themselves into whatever was near in their frantic search for soil. He opened the door slowly and called to her. The only response the waving of the vines in the breeze from the ceiling fan. He entered slowly, carefully, trying not to make too much noise. He scanned the room, looking for signs of his son. It was difficult to see, as thick, green vines covered everything, even the windows, darkening the room. The roots lining the floor made it nearly impossible to walk. He tripped and stumbled into the place where her bedside table should have been. Still, he searched the room on hands and knees, clearing away the vegetation where he could to get a better look behind the bookshelf or the dresser. He couldn't begin to pry open the closet as it was covered by a wall of creeping vines. His son could be in there, and he'd never know. He called to him, softly at first, but louder when he didn't receive an answer. His daughter stirred in her sleep, the vines wrapping tighter about the closet, the furniture. "Daddy," she said, as if from a dream of another world. He turned to her, forgetting about his son. Her thick trunk ran down the center of the bed, with so many branches, roots, and vines running from it the bed itself appeared alive, covered in so much shifting and snaking greenery.

"I'm here," he replied, lying beside his daughter. Immediately, a dozen tendrils wrapped about him, his feet, his waist, his arms, his throat. "I hate this," she said, her voice emanating from somewhere in the wood. "This thing I'm becoming."

"What thing is that?" he asked, feigning ignorance. A mistake. More vines wrapped about him.

"I'm not stupid," she said.

"I'm sorry. I know you're not." He reached out to caress her head, or at least the area where he thought her head would be. "Why do you hate it?" he asked.

"Because I'm hurting you," she replied. "Because I'm hurting the family." The vines tightened about his neck and chest.

"I understand," he tried to say, though it was more of a choked whisper.

"No you don't," she said. "You can't possibly understand." He didn't know if it was because his daughter still existed half in the dream world, but she was more lucid than she'd been in a long time. A pain like happiness stabbed through his chest.

"I haven't slept in months," he said, as if that were an answer. He tried working his right hand loose, to slip a finger or two under the vines so he could breathe a little better.

"It's like I'm in a fragment of a dream tied to another fragment," she said. "Except for everything, we're interchangeable."

"I don't understand that," he said.

"Exactly."

"I don't like myself anymore," she said.

The words knifed through his ears. He wouldn't hear them. "But you're beautiful." The vines constricted. He was lucky he'd worked his hands between them and his neck. He fought the rising panic within him. "Why do you want to hurt me?" He barely managed to speak. A particularly large branch fell across his other hand. He needed to get it free.

"Because I can," she said.

"Because you can't hurt yourself," he replied, not quite a question. Vines rose from the bed like snakes. Roots slithered and searched for anything in which to bury themselves. She was clearly agitated. While his right hand fought against the creeping vines at his throat, his left slipped around to his back pocket for the shears.

"You can fight this," he said. "I'll help you. There's got to be a way." He pulled the shears from his pocket. As if she could read his mind, a root tendril shot out and knocked them from his hand. The moment they landed, another root bound them to the floor.

"Why do you want to hurt me?" she asked.

"I don't." He almost said more, but thought better

of it.

Vine after vine wound about his legs, his arms, his body. He wouldn't be going anywhere. "You're lying," she said.

"Yes," was all he could say before the vines constricted enough that everything went black.

When he woke, her deep-sea breathing spilled over him. The bearing of unimaginable secrets hitting him like waves. Secrets that carried her farther and farther away from him. He had to stop her, if not for her sake, for his. He couldn't take more of this game, as if they were both still living. The wound in his hand throbbed, sending shooting pains up his arm. He moved to stretch it and found that it was free. In sleep, she'd released her grip. He guessed it was early evening, though he couldn't be sure. He rose to go and felt the uneven roots beneath him. Trying to be as quiet as possible, he stood, hoping his eyes would adjust, that he'd be able to see his way through the undergrowth. *Except for everything, we're interchangeable.* The voice floated somewhere in the darkness about him. Had his daughter spoken just now? No. She'd said that earlier, but what had she meant by it? He would change places with his daughter if he could. He would pull the branches from her, the thick vines, the roots. He would take them all away and graft them onto himself if he could. But would it change anything? She'd still think like a plant, still see herself as one.

He turned to her, listened to the lonely world of her breathing. He couldn't find his daughter's face now no matter how hard he tried. Even if he could penetrate the darkness, the vines that covered her hung thick. *Everything is fatal,* he thought. *We suffer in darkness* barely able to see each other. All that was left to him was to try and clear what he could. He had to do it.

He sat down again on her bed and searched for her brush in the area where the bedside table used to be, finding the handle poking out from beneath the greenery. He ran it through the vines of her hair, gently at first, so gently she dreamed of a great green valley where the wind blew over the grass. He told himself as he brushed her hair that they would get through this, that everything would be the same as it once was. He remembered his favorite picture of his daughter. She stood on the driveway of their old house in her orange hooded sweater, her blue lunchbox in hand, as she left for her first day of kindergarten, her smile a small light.

"Ow," she cried from her sleep. Her deep breathing continued unabated.

He tugged the brush through the knotted and tangled vines, determined to clear them all from her face.

"You're hurting me," she said, the sharpness of her voice cutting through sleep.

He continued until the brush caught in a knot. He pulled and pulled, but it was hopeless. "Ow!" she cried again. A leafed branch swatted at his face. "Don't worry. I know what to do," he said, panning the floor for the shears. The root that bound them held firm. He placed his heel firmly on the root and freed the shears. More branches flashed angrily about him.

"It's okay," he said, sitting again beside his daughter. "I can fix this." Gently at first, he began trimming the area around the brush, seeing if he could work it free. More vines snaked around his body. "Just give me a minute," he said. He was almost there. If he could just free the brush,

56

everything would be okay. The problem was that the branch that caught it was thick. He squeezed the shears as hard as he could, trying to cut through, but all he managed to do was get the blade stuck in a knot. "Great," he said. "I'm taking these things back tomorrow." The vines constricted around his chest. Another branch whipped dangerously close to his eyes.

"Stop!" she said.

In answer, he grabbed the branch that held the brush. "It'll only hurt for a second, I swear." He yanked with all his might, but only produced a crack. A root shot out and hit him in the head. He pulled his hand away and looked at the blood.

"Stop!" she shouted again.

"Trust me," he said. Please." He pulled on the branch again and again, but though it cracked down the middle the green fleshy fiber wouldn't give. "Goddamn it!" he yelled at last, twisting the branch back and forth until the fibers ripped one from the other. He pulled it from her head, and released the shears from its grip. She screamed. A sea of roots and branches rose up. He caught the first root as it stabbed toward him. "It's okay," he said again, as he struggled to keep hold of the root. But then one jabbed him in the ribs and another in the neck. He gasped for breath, but it wouldn't come. Another root shot at him. On instinct, he grabbed it and ripped it from her body. She screamed, even as a dozen more branches lashed out at him, tearing at his face, cutting him just below the eye. He knocked them away one after another, kicking, too, at the tendrils trying to entrap his feet. "I will not be only this," he shouted. "You will not be only this!" He swung the shears back and forth like a scythe, breaking branches, cleaving vines. It was then a sound rose from his daughter's body unlike any he'd heard before. A sound like pain, only not pain. A sound like sadness, only deeper. Like a valley burning. A valley engulfed in flames.

He ran from the room, kicking the raging roots from his feet as he went. He ran into the night and stared up into the immeasurable sky. A sky that could not protect his daughter. A sky that in fact stole his daughter from him. The wound in his hand throbbed. He worked it with his thumb, pushing at the tender flesh, understanding nothing, except the pain. He was helpless to save his daughter from what she was becoming. All he did was make it worse. And what was the point? To keep her the way he wanted, the way he remembered her? He dug deep into the wound until fire seared his arm, until he thought he understood once again who he was.

He found the duct tape in the garage and tore off long strips on his way to the swing. The cold from the hard wood plank seeped through his jeans as he worked. He wrapped the tape around his midsection then through his legs and under the swing, making a figure eight as he did so. When he was done, he tore off more strips and wrapped them around his left hand, taping it to the rope that held up one end of the swing.

It wasn't as easy as he'd remembered to get the swing started from a dead stop. How long had it been since the last time he'd gone swinging? Thirty years? Forty? He had to lean his body forward and back, pumping hard with his legs until he gained momentum. Soon, he was rising higher and higher, feet first into the blank sky. Clouds obscured the stars and even the moon had a difficult time making itself known. But it didn't matter, he'd closed his eyes anyway. He pushed the swing higher, feeling reckless, remembering what it was like to fly as a kid, remembering what it felt like not to want a thing except to soar. When he'd pushed the swing to its apex, he let go with his right hand, reaching out as if to rend the clouds, reaching for that unknown place to which his daughter had traveled, that place he'd give anywhere now to go, to be with her once again in the way they used to be. He felt nothing. No matter, he would go higher still. His legs were strong, and he had all day. He had an entire lifetime to get there. It didn't matter that he'd forgotten the feel of his wife's body as she lay beside him in bed. It didn't matter that he couldn't find his son. All he cared about was pushing the swing higher.

Then it happened. A shifting in the air about him. A slowing of black moons. For a moment, he thought maybe he'd broken free from this world, maybe something from that other place spoke to him and it would all be possible. He would know where his daughter had traveled. He held tight to that knowledge as long as he could, trying to shape it into something he could understand. A phrase. An image. Anything. But then something snapped, the swing fell from its arc and the earth rushed up to meet him. He reached out his free hand in a desperate attempt to catch that last unfathomable breath that would tell him what it meant never again to want, never again to need to hold tight to beauty that climbed like long flowers across the palm of your hand. The eyelid of the sky flickered. A flock of voices spoke to him, he was sure of it. But when his wife revived him a few hours later, all he could remember as he lay on the bed, the damp from the cold, wet grass still seeping through his jeans, was the fact that his hand hurt and nothing, nothing would ever make it right.

AT NIGHT IN CRUMBLING VOICES

Who
is invisible enough
to see you?
--Paul Celan

Prologue:

What we know of the world of the mole people is mostly conjecture. The fact of the matter is that no one who has visited their world has ever returned; or, if they have, they returned unrecognizable, even to themselves, so that they retain no memory of the past, no clue as to what might have transpired beneath the surface of our known world.

The phenomenon dates back thirty years to 1982 when a male of the species was found unconscious in the backyard sand box of Katie Fisher of Dublin, Ohio, a burgeoning suburb of Columbus. The specimen, clearly in distress, was quarantined in The Ohio State University's medical facility, where, in the brief time we were able to examine him, we learned what little we know.

Anatomically, they resemble humans, with the exception of their large and powerful digging claws, which of course have the characteristic extra thumb or prepollex. Their faces represent the only other obvious exception to their generally human resemblance with their long, pointed noses and almost invisible ears and eyes. Rumors persist of a subspecies with a protruding, pink, multi-tentacled snout, perhaps related to the "star nosed mole" or *Condylura cristata*.

Their saliva contains a neuro-toxin used for paralyzing their prey, the discovery of which has spawned a range of theories describing how the mole people have successfully managed to kidnap so many of us, leaving their victims to a fate at which we can only guess. Biologically, their blood contains a unique hemoglobin that allows them to live in low oxygen environments. Conversely, they are not able to survive for very long in our relatively rich oxygen environment—a fact we discovered tragically too late.

Though we did not have time to bring in a linguist, reports from the scientists on hand to study M., as we shall henceforth refer to him, stress that the few words he spoke bore no resemblance to any known language tree. We should point out that Drs Brady, Prilutsky, Gu, and Roy spoke eleven different languages between them, including examples from both the Sino-Tibetan and Indo European language trees (Drs Brady and Gu have since passed on). Our inability to make any significant headway with their language over these past decades has been frustrating to say the least. There is no one among us who, while on the verge of sleep, hasn't heard the voices murmuring through the earth, voices that keep us awake long into the night wishing we understood their significance. But the recent spike in the reports of these voices combined with the rise in the number of kidnappings has changed considerably the way top officials view the crisis. State and local governments have given the matter the highest priority. Even now, a team of linguists is working around the clock to find a primer for their language based on the recordings of M.'s smattering of speech thirty years ago, and recent articles suggest that a breakthrough will come any day now.

It is unfortunate that M. succumbed to Oxygen Toxicity Syndrome within forty-eight hours of his capture. There is much we could have learned from him. Still, we maintain a positive outlook, remembering that before the discovery of M. we had no definitive proof of the existence of the mole people, only myth and superstition. While we have yet to discover the reason for their hold on us, many in the scientific community feel we are approaching a watershed moment.

Richard Hubbard

Dawn and silence. How you, then, a boy scarcely thirteen wake to find swollen in your hand and wet. Snot colors the image. What is this? What is this? Not rain. Not milk for cereal. Not pus from the dog's eye. It smells of Sunday cleaning. Richard, will you mop the kitchen? Swish. Swish goes the bleach water over the floor and down the hall. Follow it to the bathroom where you wash. But your underwear proves sticky. Ungenial summer continually reminding of wetness. You rush away from such odious handwork and return to your bed. Soft sheets touching. One magazine after another filters through your hands. Lush jungle of hair falls black over sultry eyes. Lips parted, unraveling. Angelic sheen of soda water breasts. Dark airbrushed sea curls between coastlines of skin. The mystery of the universe. Ceaseless tangle of ocean. Wet. Wet. Undeniably wet!

Such errors prove catastrophic.

The photograph ruffles into dream. The coarse and crenellated features of a man's hand stroking, stroking. Tree threads sky. You lean against it and imagine you're ... What is this? What is this? Your sky rises within. Clouds bursting between your legs. You want to touch it, to hold it. Hold the man. You watch as he puts the piccolo to his pursed lips and walks down the path to the graveled lot. You follow, not knowing why, only that you must. Wash your face of virtue. Explode the bomb hidden beneath your shirt. Bear your true skin to the sun.

How then a boy scarcely thirteen wakes to find swollen in his hand and wet.

It's 3 a.m. The broken hour. Lie on your back and listen. Fold the pillow over your ears if you must. The words still come, unstoppered.

Police Report #1
Detective: Bill Carpenter
Transcribed from the Voice Recorder:
  Corner of Broadway and Main
29, Oct, 2012, 10pm.

Due to the predominance of disappearances in this sector, I've positioned my car for the best possible vantage of the houses around and about Skyline Park.

The only consistency between each case is that the subjects disappear after going to bed. In some cases, a spouse wakes and rolls over only to find a slight depression in the bed where the beloved once slept. In other cases, a child stumbles sleepy-eyed into the room, calling for their mommy or daddy only to find an empty bed.

She left me seven months ago. She shook me awake, and when I opened my eyes, she told me she no longer loved me. That same weekend she packed her bags and left. The divorce papers came in the mail yesterday, the only hint she still existed at all. After she left, I took the pictures off the walls and shelves and put them in a box in the closet. When that didn't help, I rearranged the furniture and started sleeping on the couch. After six months, I sold the furniture and moved to the other side of town. Still, I can't rid myself of her memory. Sometimes, I find myself talking to her when I'm in the car. I look to the passenger seat, and I see her. I know she's not there, but it doesn't matter. I see her all the same.

Minimal movement in and out of the houses along

Broadway and Main. Nothing suspect. A couple teenagers making out in the park, a few people arriving home late, but no one leaving. Each car hostage in the driveway until the next morning. Yet at least once a week there is another disappearance.

We used to like to drive. It didn't matter where. We would just get in the car and drive. She'd take off her shoes, lean the seat back, and put her feet on the dash. I loved her feet. The curve of them. The way she wiggled her toes when she was happy. Some of our best conversations occurred in that car. A 2003 Corolla. We talked about having kids. She wanted three. We talked about where we'd retire. I thought Mexico would be nice. We talked about what we might have done if we could start all over again. She would have become a marine biologist. I thought we talked about everything. I thought I knew her inside and out.

The nature of absence is a mystery.

Melissa Morton

Deep in your breath sits a dimly lit stage. You wake and wait for the red dress to spin. A tornado of flame. Of afternoon sun. Vortex of cardinals. The minutes stretch under the night sky.

Your parents had to bring you as it's impossible to find a sitter in a foreign country. How could they know the red dress would spin fire in your brain? That the ruins of this ancient stage would build scaffolding in your body? The guitarist's hands circle back on themselves. Shadow swirling on the edge of light. The cracking rhythm of cypress and spruce. She steps from the darkness. The lady in red. Can you see? your mother asks. A dark cloud of curly black hair hovers before you. Yes, you tell her. Yes, I see. Your legs see. Your hands see. With each slap of the palmas, you see more clearly. With each strike of the dancer's heels, you are unmoored from the blindness. See yourself now, floating

Red

is a

river

   flow

ing

between

light
and
dark

between

ordinary
and the
clapping
in
your
body

You don't sleep any more. You haven't in three years. Try wine. Gin. Nothing keeps us out for long. Shout at us! Tell us to fall back through the ground we came from. Tell us you are no longer that girl. You have forgotten who that girl was. We have no ears to hear.

Lecture One: Mythology of the Hollow Earth

In order to better understand the mythology and speculation that has built up around the mole people, we have asked Dr. Frank Baxter, Professor of English at the University of Southern California, to supply us with a series of lectures on the subject. The first of these lectures discusses the mythology behind the hollow earth theory. The following and all subsequent lectures are taken verbatim from Dr. Baxter's notes:

Descents to the underworld have long been a part of mythology from Osiris and Odysseus to Gilgamesh, from Aeneas and Orpheus to Jesus, and on down the line to the Anglo Saxon hero, Beowulf, but the descent itself is not our topic today. Rather, it is the ubiquitous nature of hollow earth imagery in mythology that concerns us here. The Greeks speak of Hades; Norse mythology refers to svartalfheim; the Jewish faith to Sheol; the Vedic texts of Ancient India to Shamballa; the Christian Old Testament to Hell; Buddhists talk of the city of Agartha, which exists at the earth's core; ancient Celtic mythology speaks of the cave of the Cruachan from which strange creatures emerge; ancient legends from the Angami Naga tribe in India, or the Taíno from the Caribbean, or the Iroquois in North America, or the indigenous peoples of Brazil all speak of ancestors who emerged from inside the earth.

Why is it that every culture known to man has legends of a world beneath the surface of our own? Why does there seem to be a compelling need for heroes to make a journey to that world and return to tell the tale? The noted Swiss psychiatrist, Carl Jung, talks of the importance of the unconscious, of connecting to the "lower stories of the skyscraper." He mentions that since the Age of Reason we've disconnected from that which is invisible, suggesting that what we cannot see may be more important than what we can.

Of late, some anthropologists have put forward the claim that these ubiquitous stories of descent are evidence of the mole people's influence dating back to the dawn of human civilization. Dr. Abe, the most noted of these "molopogists," as they've come to be known, goes so far as to claim that cultural representations of such heroes as Orpheus or Beowulf are necessary not simply to re-connect us with Jung's "lower stories of the skyscraper," but also to defend us from what we are sure to find there. In other words, at an unconscious level, we fear the mole people and what they represent. Dr. Abe's current theoretical work proposes that it is precisely this fear that leads to our secret desire to enslave them. In his seminal paper entitled, "Of Slaves and Skyscrapers: Why We Need Heroes," published in *American Anthropologist* in 2006, he posits the prevalence of superheroes in modern movies, video games, and comic books as a desperate attempt to keep the mole people at bay. At present, his work has been limited to pop culture. Of course, there is as yet no evidence of an actual slave ring involving the mole people. This lack of evidence has hurt his reputation among hardcore scientists. Still, his ideas resonate with lay people and some in the scientific community.

Annie Clarkson

You live in a shell. Or rather, you live a second life there. The first visible to the world. The second not even to yourself. Neither life decidable. The spiral-shaped life began with a kiss, a kiss in a garden, a garden in a park at night beneath dark stars. What thin-skinned redemption! If you try to walk your way out of the shell, say on your breath, your skin bleeds a thousand cuts. And so you sit in the center, exactly six inches of space between yourself and the spiraling wall. Here, you tend your two children and husband. Rise before dawn and make their lunches. Set out their clothes and get them up. Walk them to the bus stop. Kiss your recently risen husband when you return. Then wait. You can be very small when you wait. Curled tight. A dormouse in daily hibernation. You don't uncurl until your children come home from school. Even then you draw a circle about yourself. You'd be surprised what you can do inside a circle inside a shell. You can tell your children to practice their music and do their homework. You can read to them and make them a snack. Prepare dinner and practice piano with them after. You can tuck them in at night before dripping into your trim womb. You can even make love to your husband. Then rise again the next morning and start over. What you cannot do is think of the kiss. Better to beat your head against the sharp edges of the shell. Let the blood run to your lips and lick it away. What you cannot do is step out of the circle. Try and you'll find the tether tied to your ankle that always pulls you back. You tied it yourself. It's much more effective if you do it that way. Less chance of slipping out. Less chance of slipping. Less chance of

Sleeping pills won't stop us. They only distort dreams already unracked by reason. Keep your eyes open, gaped pores absorbing the darkness. Waiting. Waiting. Watching. For what? You know very well for what.

Police Report #2
Detective: Bill Carpenter
Transcribed from the Voice Recorder
30, Oct, 2012.

There have been two hundred fifty-three complaints about the voices to date. That's up twenty-two percent from last year and thirty percent from the year before that. It doesn't take a rocket scientist to see the pattern. I would also add as anecdotal evidence that people seem more agitated. The voices are getting to them, though they won't admit it. When did people in this town ever admit to weakness? They'll stare you straight in the eye and say they're doing fine even when their lives are falling apart around them. Richard Hubbard as much as said that yesterday morning when I bumped into him at the coffee shop.

"Don't see you in here often," I said.

"Oh, needed a little pick me up today," he replied.

That's it. End of story. He was hearing the night voices. I guarantee.

After analyzing current data, I've come up with a series of questions:

1. Are the voices getting louder?
2. Why are they increasing in frequency, coming nearly every night now?
3. What determines who hears the voices and who doesn't? (It will be difficult to find conclusive data as psychologists have suggested hearing the voices is vastly under-reported. Our own staff psychologist suggests eighty-

percent go unreported. If this is true, it means nearly everyone has heard them at one point or another.)

4. What is the relationship between the voices and the rash of disappearances? (The data seems to indicate there is a relationship. The more voices we hear, the more people disappear. That said, no definite connection has yet been made between those who hear the voices and those who disappear, as the disappeared are never around to corroborate.)

Note: I don't buy the superstition about the mole people. Talk of human size moles rising out of the earth at night only to steal people away into their burrows for God knows what purpose. It doesn't make sense. I'm a man of science. Occam's razor. All things being equal, the simplest answer is the best answer, and mole people are not a simple answer. Dig into people's lives a bit. Tunnel into their past, into their relations, and you'll find out where they've gone. Most of the time a so-called "disappearance" is nothing more than John or Sally running away because they need to escape something at home, or because they've taken up with a new lover.

Sometimes, when I'm deep into the facts of another person's life, I wonder what it might be like to disappear myself. When I was young, my favorite movies were those old, road movies with Bing Crosby and Bob Hope. *Road to Morocco, Road to Zanzibar, Road to Singapore,* to *Rio,* to *Bali,* and *Hong Kong.* If I saw one of those movies was going to be on TV, I'd play hooky from school. If one of those movies was on TV right now, I might never come back to work. Yes, I can see the attraction. We don't need mole people to explain why someone wants a new life. I sure as hell don't need them to tell me why Beth left. Sure our relationship was going a bit stale. After fifteen years, what relationship doesn't? She'd lost interest in sex, but she said it had nothing to do with me. We liked to do the same things. Going out for dinner and drinks. Sometimes dancing. I'll never forget the time she tried to teach me the meringue. I threw my hip out and landed on the floor. We laughed about it all the way home.

I don't know why she left. I'll never know why. I don't understand anything.

David Singer

Spiders spin suppers while you sip whiskey and surf porn. It's two in the morning. Time to be the one on whom nothing is lost. It's two in the morning. Time for the taking of a toast and tea. It's two in the morning. But this press of time—take it a little thing next to what endures. All this hurrying soon will be over.

A windowpane in a window frame holds back the wind. You sip your whiskey. A door in a dry desert keeps out the dirt. You sip your whiskey. A cap covers the container. You sip your whiskey and rise when the morning shrieks your name to bury others whose game has ended. The irony does not escape you. It is a family business. There is irony there, too, if only you could find it. Keep the sun chained to the floor. You will dress in darkness. Keep the light bolted to the door. You will eat your cereal in darkness. Keep the sky locked inside the umbrella. Let it retain its birds. You will drive to work in darkness. Keep the trees fastened to the grave. You have lost your crown of feathers. Time to prepare the dead in darkness.

The box is eighty-four inches long, twenty-eight inches wide, and twenty-three high. A coffin not of your creation. You found yourself in it twelve years ago, when you agreed to quit your studies and run the family business. Your parents were ill. Your sister raising her children. One year, you said. One year to get the business back on its feet, and then I'm gone. Off to graduate school. Off to study poetry. Delayed till she had ceased to know. Delayed till in its vest of snow. Delayed. A flick of the wrist and the birds are dead.

You sleep so little your mind can scarcely function. You're beginning to understand what it means to die. Go ahead! Stare out the window of the embalming room. Look out over the gravestones. What separates you from the dead? What is life if you don't feel anything?

Lecture Two: The Hollow Earth in Science
Dr. Frank Baxter, USC

The second Astronomer Royal in Britain, Edmund Halley (1656-1742), was the first to put forth the hollow earth theory in 1692. He said the earth was 800 miles thick with two inner concentric shells and an innermost core. Each shell had its own atmosphere and magnetic poles. Further, he speculated the Aurora Borealis was created by gas leaking from the atmosphere inside the earth.

Nearly one hundred and thirty years later, an American Army officer and amateur scientist named John Cleve Symmes (1779-1829) took up where Halley left off, expounding his own hollow earth theory on the American lecture circuit in 1818. He called his theory, "Cellular Cosmogony." Like Halley, he conceived the earth as a shell about 800 miles thick with openings at the poles. Further, he conceived of four inner shells also with openings at their poles. Symmes himself never wrote a book of his ideas, as he was too busy expounding them on the lecture circuit, but others did.

Perhaps the most interesting of the hollow earth theorists was an American physician and alchemist turned messiah named Cyrus Teed (1839-1908). Obsessed with discovering the potential for electricity, Teed was badly shocked during an experiment. While unconscious, he had a revelation from God. When he awoke, he changed his name to Koresh and expounded the religion of "Koreshanity," part of which involved a hollow earth cosmology where the earth and sky exist inside a sphere and the sun is a simple battery operated device. In the 1870's, he established a commune in New York. Other communes of his followers rose up in Chicago, San Francisco, and Florida.

These men and others like them were the founding fathers of hollow earth science, but the work is by no means limited to science. Over time, the theory insinuated its way into spiritualism and the occult. In 1906, William Reed continued its development in his book, *Phantom of the Poles,* wherein he asserts that the poles themselves are phantoms that can never be reached. In 1907, Lady Paget Walburga (a close friend of Queen Victoria) expounded the hollow earth theory, claiming that cities existed beneath a desert, one of which was where the inhabitants of Atlantis moved. She claimed we would find the openings to this world in the 21st century. Note that while others before her in both science and literature talked of monsters, dinosaurs, and floating cats beneath the earth, Lady Walburga is the first to claim the existence of a lost civilization. Over the last hundred years, countless spiritualists, many of whom claimed to have made astral journeys to the underworld to speak with the inhabitants there, have championed her work. Strangely, none of these spiritualists has mentioned the mole people, talking instead of ancient Sumeria, Troy, Atlantis, Maya, Assyria, and El Dorado. Though most contemporary scientists have dismissed these spiritualists' claims, the recent public clamor has led a rising number of scientists to take another look at these spiritualist reports, combing them for any hint or mention of the mole people. While the results are inconclusive, the sheer number of "eye witness" accounts of denizens inhabiting the deepest regions of the earth gives one pause. When these accounts are combined with the rise of the "subterranean fiction" and "lost world" genres in literature, it doesn't take much of a leap to find substantial anecdotal evidence to support the current hysteria over the mole people. But that topic will have to wait for the next lecture.

Mary Pollard

Somebody's calling for you. Calling again. Don't tell me who. You know who. Don't tell me why. You know why.

Blood curtsies in front of your house. Blood you won't wash away because you keep running. Sit still a moment and listen to the pumping of your heart when you were fourteen. Listen to the circumstance of your breath on that crisp October morning. Hear your sister, Ellen's breath, tangled with your own.

"I want to ride first."

"No, me!"

"Okay, Ellen, you can go first."

Now that same voice screams through your mind like the mouth of a kettle.

"But what am I going to do?" *Ellen asks.*

"Whatever you do, don't let loose. Don't let loose."

She tied the reins around her waist.

Since then it's as if you've been looking through etched glass. Or tracing your life in wax. What's left is a language not your own. A language designed to conceal. "I'm sorry," is your primer. "Why wasn't it me?" your Rosetta Stone. The moon calls to you but all you hear is your sister's scream as the horse dragged her down the street.

So you sit, spinning coins, counting the times it falls on tails, slipping through the gray.

Spin One: Marry a man who is nothing like you. A man whose only concern is to make lots of money. The less you have, the more alive you feel.

Spin Two: Have a child. Now you have an excuse to sleep.

Spin Three: Have another. Now you have no excuse.

For twenty years, the last face you saw when you went to bed was your sister Ellen's. For twenty years, the first face you saw when you woke was hers. You have given her enough. Punished yourself enough. Listen to the voices rising within.

We are holding your sky.

Police Report #3
Detective: Bill Carpenter
Transcribed from the Voice Recorder
6, Nov, 2012.

I completed my interview with Dr. Miles Tishner regarding his purported attempted kidnapping. He appeared clear headed, surprisingly so for a professor. Personal experience has shown they talk circles around you if you enter the narrow sphere of their particular field. You've got to be careful or you'll get lost in the rabbit hole yourself. Dr. Tishner's field is philosophy of the mind. He told me after the interview that I might not even exist. I might be a construction of his mind. A dream! I smiled politely and asked what made him so sure I wasn't dreaming him.

The subject reported that he woke last night at approximately one-thirty a.m. to the sound of digging in his bedroom, a digging he described as "not normal." The subject reports he was so frightened he couldn't move from his bed. I asked if he opened his eyes at this point, but he said he wasn't sure. He reports only that the next thing he knew a cold, six-fingered hand slipped over his mouth. Subject reports that he tried to get up but that the more he exerted himself the tighter the grip held him. It was then, he reports, a gravelly voice whispered in his ear: *Unbraid your hair for it is time to swim!*

I asked if he knew what the voice meant, and he replied that he had no idea. I find this fact suspicious. Stranger still, he says the voice asked if he would come willingly. He reports that when he replied, "No, I have a book to finish writing on Cartesian dualism," the kidnapper swept him up in two powerful arms and hurried him toward the pit in the closet. I asked if he was able to get a good look at his kidnapper at this point, but the subject simply replied that it was too dark. Note: I find this difficult to believe. I told him as much, and the subject amended his earlier statement to say that a little voice inside his head warned him not to look. I asked if it was the same voice that told him to braid his hair. He said that it was in fact his own voice issuing the warning. I don't pretend to understand.

It is at this point that the subject's quick thinking seems to have saved him. As the kidnapper attempted to drag the subject into the pit, the subject grabbed a cane buried in the corner behind his tweed jackets. The kidnapper pulled the subject into the hole, feet first, but, quite by accident, the cane got caught in the opening. Like a stick in the mouth of a lion. The subject reports that at this point the kidnapper yanked on the subject's feet to no avail. Frustrated, the kidnapper released his grip. That's when the subject says he kicked the kidnapper in the nose, much as one might do to an attacking shark. When I questioned the professor on why he was so specific about kicking his assailant in the nose when he'd previously stated that he couldn't see, the professor grew sullen and quickly changed the subject.

The professor went on to describe the howl of pain that rose from the depths of the tunnel. He went so far as to use the words, "inhuman howl." He reports that following this "inhuman howl" he climbed quickly out of the pit and ran straight to his car where he promptly drove to his colleague's house, one Victor Cooper, with whom he plays ping pong twice weekly.

This morning's investigation confirms the pit in Prof. Tishner's closet. However, a large rock blocked any attempt by this investigator to follow the tunnel for more than a few feet. Forensic reports confirm that the rock had to have been placed in the tunnel from someone below the surface. Note: This doesn't rule out the possibility that Prof. Tishner could have climbed into the tunnel, blocked the entrance to his bedroom with a boulder from the other side, then exited the tunnel at some still unknown location.

The question remains as to whether Prof. Tishner is lying, and if so, why. I don't have an answer, only the feeling that he is avoiding the truth. He knows what that voice meant. Possibly even who said it. And he must have caught a glimpse of the face. I trust my instincts. It follows, of course, that if he lied about even one fact, he is capable of lying about everything. I'd lie, too, if I'd dug a hole in the floor of my closet, a hole that leads to a secret place created from my own mind. If Prof. Tishner is capable of dreaming me, he's certainly capable of dreaming a world beneath the surface of the earth. A place where no case will go unsolved because you can dream the solution. A place that contains everything you never had, everything you hoped you'd find in Zanzibar, Morocco, Rio, and Singapore. A place where your wife waits for you. Where she's still your wife. The woman who loved you. Not some other woman who left. Then you wouldn't need movies. You wouldn't need a job that takes you into other people's lives, lives you spend too much time inhabiting because you want to escape your own. It wouldn't be too hard to dig a hole in your bedroom closet and make it look like it had been dug from the other side. Finding a suitable boulder to block the hole would be a small price to pay for the knowledge that the place existed, that beyond that rock there was a tunnel that led to a place where the dream you've played over and over in your mind might actually be real.

Richard Hubbard

The magazines collect like dead wasps beneath your bed. And you are a pile of stones to bury them. Build your battlements, shovel dirt to fortify the holds. In command now of nothing save emptiness. Time inches by. Choose your gun, sir! Choose! What will it be? Not a woman. No. They are dead and gone. Stick figures rising from the earth are too easily shot down. Loosen the tourniquet about your waist until you are found out, until you can breathe deeply enough to understand your own song.

What made you sign up for acting class your parents will never understand. But you did, chiseling away at the stone. A heroic act! You and Kevin the only two boys in the class. Fast friends. Whirlwind friends. You didn't go anywhere without him until the night both worlds stood open. There you are lying beside him in bed, spinning the secret thread of dreams. Watch as his hand braids the few hairs on your chest before descending. Wait, unsure, as you swell inside the brilliance of his hand. He whispers your name, but you don't answer. Lost in twilight, the place between. Is it not time for the stone to bloom? Time to speak of wounded things?

But there is an owl making a bed of brambles in your heart, shredding and clawing until you can no longer breathe. His hand falls away, and you roll over to the edge of the bed. Your back like a crooked wing, jailing. You dream of sand and water, of a shore older than waiting.

Yet, that's all you do is wait. You lie in bed, wading through the hot cement of hours, while the voices kiss the child you once were. Pull your hands from the frozen sea and reach out for the man you are. Why wait and wonder if the voices will carry you home?

Lecture Three: The Hollow Earth in Literature
Dr. Frank Baxter, USC

Almost as if in support of hollow earth science, references in literature have long been a part of our heritage, stepping out of the classical era and into the middle ages with *Beowulf,* Dante's *Inferno,* and even Milton's *Paradise Lost,* and on into the eighteenth century with Holberg's *Nicolai Klimii iter subteranneum* or Casanova's eighteen hundred page epic, *Icosaméron.* However, it is not until the nineteenth and twentieth centuries that the genre of what we shall call "subterranean" and/or "lost world" fiction really begins to flower.

Poe's *Narrative of Arthur Gordon Pym* in 1838 mentions a subterranean labyrinth complete with hieroglyphs describing a secret "region to the south." From Poe, we can move quickly through the last half of the nineteenth century and the early twentieth with Verne's *Journey to the Center of the Earth* (1864), Carroll's *Alice in Wonderland* (1865), Haggard's *King Solomon's Mines* (1885), Frank L. Baum's *Oz* books (1900-1921), Conan Doyle's *The Lost World* (1912), Edgar Rice Burroughs' *At the Earth's Core* (1914) and *The Land that Time Forgot* (1918), Hilton's *Lost Horizon* (1933), Cooper's *King Kong* (1933), and Lovecraft's *At the Mountains of Madness* (1936). One can't help but wonder if nighttime visits from the mole people somehow wormed their way into the unconscious imaginings of these writers. If so, we owe a debt of gratitude to them, and must remember this when other shriller voices call for their extermination.

However, this early flowering of the genre proved to be premature compared with the full bloom that occurred in the latter half of the twentieth century and on up to today, beginning with C.S. Lewis' *The Silver Chair* (1953), Tolkien's *The Lord of the Rings* (1954-55), and on to Cameron's *The Mountains at the Bottom of the World* (1972), Crichton's *Congo* (1980), McCoy's *Indiana Jones and the Hollow Earth* (1997), Long's *The Descent* (1999), Cook's *Abduction* (2000), Farren's *Underland* (2002), Robinson's *Arntarktos Rising* (2007), and Johnson's *Pym* (2011). The list is by no means an exhaustive one, particularly as it only covers the genre in literature while the dominant popular art form of the latter half of the twentieth century is clearly the cinema. However, to list the movies that exhibited this mytheme would take more space than is allotted for this lecture. Suffice it to say, the importance of the "lost world" and/or "subterranean fiction" genre cannot be overstated. What is less clear is the relationship between this genre and the influence of the mole people.

The most significant study on the subject was conducted by the Department of Psychiatry at Harvard University Medical School over a ten-year period from 1996 to 2006. Though the scientists involved admit the near impossibility of controlling for every variable, the evidence is startling. What the Harvard study indicated was that in the months prior to nearly every book publication and even more clearly before every movie premiere, there was a significant spike in the number of people who reported lack of sleep due to hearing the voices of the mole people. The evidence is most startling in the months prior to the release of *Batman Begins* (2005), with its infamous cave scene. Though the Harvard study reaches no conclusions, it clearly suggests a pattern well worth further research. The question for future scientists is whether or not the voices led to the creation of the mytheme in these movies and books, or whether they simply lead people to seek the mytheme out where it appears.

Melissa Morton

It's always winter in Ohio, snowdrifts piling over your eyes. No matter where you cast your gaze, there is no fertile ground. But there are pockets, tiny sheaves of hope hidden in cities. At thirteen you find a flamenco class, but it is across town, nearly a forty-minute drive. Your parents enroll you in a jazz class closer to home.

It's difficult to rein the dark clouds that gather. Try as you might, they bulge and billow across your horizon. Don't fight it. Better to let the frost design you. Better to disappear in the morning's dew. Better to hobble through the hail of years than slip on black ice. There are worse things than not dancing. At least that's what you tell yourself. Better to stay inside and be one of those who hear the rain.

Numbers have their own music. Differential equations may not dance but they can detail the body's movement. Polygons and Polytopes convey the truth of a body's pose. You have an ear for advanced mathematics even if your body listens to other rhythms. So, when you enroll in college as an engineer, there is no longer anyone to fight. We're so proud of you, your parents say. We're so pleased with you, your teachers say. You're doing the right thing, you say to yourself.

After work, you walk into the cratered evening. Drink deep of the hollow night, not daring to touch the dew of your own desire. The wind calls, and still you keep your head lowered. The light of the moon turns, and still you will not climb out of yourself. You dare not taste the memory of storm.

You fear the darkness that bruises. What if you open the door in the night and no one is there? No one except the

93

wind and so much glass, jangling. What if your life is only a stuttered scar and not fit for dancing at all?

We are coming. Our hands slipping free of earth. We are coming. You will know soon enough.

Police Report #4
Detective: Bill Carpenter
Private Report—Unfiled
9, Nov, 2012.

They found dirt in Melissa Morton's bedroom. A hole in her bedroom closet with a big pile of dirt next to it and tracks in the carpet leading up to her bed. The forensics experts are examining photos of the scene. But you don't need an expert to tell you some kind of big animal made those tracks. An animal unlike anything I've ever encountered before. More like some creature from the Pliocene. The tracks showed five toes with long, clearly identifiable claws. Based on the size of those hind limbs, I don't ever want to see the forelimbs. Your typical mole's forelimbs have ten times the strength of a man. Imagine the strength of a human size mole. The strange thing is there was no sign of a struggle. Just those tracks of dirt walking up to the bed. The covers pulled back like she was getting up for her morning ritual. Not a trace of blood. No human footprints indicating she might have walked away on her own. She simply disappeared. Rumors are flying that the mole people eat you whole. They pick you up in their giant fore claws, paralyze you with their venom, then swallow you down.

The truth is I sometimes hope that's what happened to Beth. I combed our place up and down after she left, looking for the slightest trace of dirt. I told myself for a long time that it could have been the mole people. I told myself they were too smart to leave any trace. How do you think they've been living beneath us for thousands of years? They'd have been hunted down long ago if they weren't smarter than we are. But now I don't know.

The brass sealed off the scene fast. I'm the chief inspector assigned to these disappearances, and after the initial assessment, I wasn't even allowed in. At least I got a picture of the tracks, the hole.

Something wasn't right. I've been on the force long enough to know what's what. Sometimes I think there's more cops on the wrong side of the law than the right. So I staked out the crime scene. Parked my car down the street and watched. Within two hours of the report, they had a dump truck filled with dirt on the victim's driveway. They were taking wheelbarrow after wheelbarrow full of dirt into the bedroom. Only one reason I can think to do that. They wanted to fill up that hole and fill it up good. And only one reason they'd want to fill up that hole. They don't want anyone coming out or going in.

I went to Sam's Tavern after. Drank away what was left of the afternoon. I caught myself showing the picture to the other drunks at the bar, letting slip that I'd seen the same tracks the morning Beth disappeared but had been too bereaved to make note of it. I keep staring at that photo, and the more I look at it the more I'm sure I did see some faint traces of dirt in our room that morning. Dark, rich dirt. The kind of dirt you only find deep beneath the surface of the earth. Yeah. There was dirt all over our bedroom. I'm sure of it now.

Annie Clarkson

The banging of the door echoes the banging in your head. Or is it the other way around? And if the door opens? Will you say you've made a horrible mistake, and you cannot live without him? No.

You wait in your car on the curb before your lover's house. The hours splinter. The path to the porch weeps large. Speak yourself free! Release the hand that trembles as it grasps your heart. Unlock the silence where your lover sits. Move through the snow that drifts around your words.

You wait. The snow falls, naming the hour. The glacier too vast to cross. And so you sit, sundered from the only world that ever mattered. Each flake that falls another night. Each flake another death. Each flake a breath you hold, waiting for the right words to speak. But they do not come. Not even the dead, who speak with tongues of longing, can make sense of crumbling words.

And so you sit.
And wait.
And he doesn't come out.
And you don't go in.
And time carries the words to dust.

Except the word you left on your shuttered lids. Please.

It sounds like a distant bell. One you can never answer. Because you have made your choice. Rise before dawn and make their lunches. Set out their clothes and get them up. Walk them to the bus stop. Kiss your recently risen husband when you return. Then wait.

Wait a thousand years if need be. Wait while your house of skin is tortured. Wait until you are the space between the flame, until you can endure the burning.

Lecture Four: The Language of the Mole People
Dr. Frank Baxter, USC

Though M., the only mole person to have been caught and studied, was unconscious for forty of the forty-eight hours of his captivity, Drs' Brady, Prilutsky, Gu, and Roy were able to record five articulations they believed to be words spoken either while the subject was unconscious, as in the case of: *Gamine* and *Seruc,* or once the subject woke, as in the case of: *Dersac, Mepos* and *Fler.*

It has not been an easy task, as even a casual perusal of the scholarship will indicate. The first linguist to attempt a primer was Dr. Svalnyack, whose ultimate contribution after six years of work was a book explaining why it was impossible to crack the language of the mole people. Not to be deterred, Dr. Negribe took up where Svalnyack left off, theorizing that his predecessor's failures had to do with an emphasis on morphology and syntax as opposed to phonology. At first, Dr. Negribe's research created quite a stir as he paired the five known words with the five movements of Brahms Third Piano Sonata—the only piano sonata with five movements, which had long been seen as an anomaly in and of itself. His work involved meditating on the appropriate word while listening to the sonata, a different word for each movement. The results were fascinating, though regrettably not particularly illuminating, as no primer emerged. It wasn't until Dr. Greene took up the call in the late 1990's that real progress seemed to have been made. Dr. Greene theorized that though Negribe's research was in the end misguided, it was based on an important fundamental principle. In short, Dr. Greene argued that

M.'s articulations were not "words" as we understand them but complex ideas and feelings, in this way closer to Egyptian hieroglyphs or even Chinese characters. Dr. Greene's contributions to the field cannot be overstated as they mark a turning point in the search for a primer.

A few short years later, Dr. LeMarck continued Greene's and Negribe's promising research, suggesting that while M.'s language shared certain tonal properties with music (particularly Brahms) its logic had more in common with poetry, particularly poetry's ability to contain paradox. The history of science is nothing if not the history of the slow accumulation of knowledge, as one scientist builds on the work of another until a tipping point is reached. That tipping point occurred in 2007 with Drs. Headley and Ishiguro and their genius in understanding that the organizing principle of the mole people's language must be metaphor itself. From their groundbreaking work, a basic primer was established.

For a brief taste, please see below:

"Gamine"—if used on its own can be roughly translated as "flute of night," but when combined with "Seruc" means "the dead speak in order to live."

"Mepos"—on its own appears to mean, "Look with tears/words," but combined with "Dersac" means "weep away your wall of stone." However, when combined with "Fler" could be translated as, "Give your words shadow to spread over the world."*

The richness and flexibility of the mole people's language should be clear from even this small sample. Though we do not as yet have a comprehensive understanding of the language, linguists generally agree that its unique ability to hold paradox makes it worthy of further study. The scientific community remains hopeful that we will have the opportunity to put theory to practice when and if we have a chance to come in contact with the mole people once again.

> *Note: there has been much recent scholarly debate over this last translation. Dr. LeMarck agrees with Headley and Ishiguro's translation, but in an essay appearing in the two thousand and eight issue of *Linguistics* Dr. Trentner argues for a slightly different translation: "Give your shadow to spread over the world as words." Further, he postulates that whether you say "Mepos fler" or "Fler mepos" determines the meaning. The debate has yet to be decided.

David Singer

The thinner you grow the less people know you. Maybe then you can escape the business. But the mortuary shrinks around you until not even Alice could exit this door. Look out the mail slot and wait for the applications. One by one, they drop. One by one you read through the shimmering swell of words. A PhD in poetry! A life of letters! One by one you throw them in the trash. Same as last year. And the year before that. Shadow-stripped you return to your casket to wait morning. It is smaller than it was yesterday. Both the casket and the morning.

Remember the venomed hours that put you to sleep? The marks of responsibility pock your face. Words are the only antidote. Words that sing. Words that snap at your heels until you wake. Where are they? Harvest them. Cut them from the page if you must. Pin them on the walls of your casket. Press them like thyme to your eyes. Do not cellar the soul.

Still you wither, blindness to grave. Your roots dried. Your stem a husk, windblown over the draught-colored river that weaves through your death.

Follow it.

Let your mouth thirst.

Beat your way along the walls. Do you hear the hollow parts? The weak parts where you can break through? It takes a strong fist, night-toughened hands to punch past the partition.

The lines you've written on the inside of your casket blind. False words only lead you farther away. Come to us with parched lips. Come on your hands to us. Let your voice crumble into the night, then follow the trail.

Carry the map in your mouth. The time is coming when you will unfold it. Soon, we will pull you from this frozen room into the earth.

Police Report #5
Detective: Bill Carpenter
Transcribed from the Voice Recorder;
  corner of First and North Pearl
13, Nov, 2012.

There were ten to twelve in the group, made up mostly of men, though I counted at least three women. Each dressed in a hoodie and carrying a bat or some type of yard implement: a hoe, rake, or shovel. They weren't going to be doing any gardening at two-thirty in the morning, I was sure of that. So, I left my car and followed them. It became obvious within minutes that they were some kind of vigilante group, as they methodically moved up one street and down another, splitting into two groups when they needed to cover an alleyway, then meeting up again when the alley joined the street.

I've always been good in math, so it didn't take long to figure ground zero of their search. They were working a pattern of three square city blocks with Melissa Morton's house at the center, working from the outside in so that they could close off anything caught inside.

I could appreciate their method even if I didn't approve. They had a pattern. Something you could see, plan on. You could prepare a strategy. Maybe Beth had a plan, too. Maybe I just wasn't aware of it. You know what they say. If you want a good haircut, don't marry a barber. Same with a detective. We never see the clues close to home. It's hard to think I was that oblivious. Better to believe she shut me out. That one day she simply woke and closed the door between us. Locked it and threw away the key. I never had a chance after that.

They wouldn't have caught the teenage boy before he'd snuck in the back door of his house if he hadn't fumbled the lock. It was the clanging of the key on the cement that alerted them. They swarmed on him before I could fire my gun over their heads. That got their attention.

"What the hell are you all doing?" I shouted, flashing my badge. "This boy did nothing."

"He's one of them!" someone shouted.

"One of what?"

A man stepped forward, and I shined my light in his eyes. It was Willard Clayton. I'd known him for years. His wife had been friends with Beth. We'd never talked about what happened. I wondered what he knew. "One of what, Willard?" I repeated.

"One of them mole people." He clearly meant what he said. The others nodded their heads in agreement.

"Have you all gone nuts?" I asked, parting the crowd with my flashlight. I knelt beside the boy and used my kerchief to wipe away the blood from his face. He moaned at my touch. "Are you all satisfied?" I asked. "You nearly killed a teenage kid."

They shook their heads in disbelief, then started to back away, a few of them fleeing into the night. Willard stood over the boy, his mouth agape, as I put the cuffs on him. "It can't be," he kept repeating.

I didn't want to admit how often I'd said those same words. It was as if I'd never known her. As if the person I thought I knew was a façade.

I don't hear the voices of the mole people like most of the town. But I still can't sleep. I wake up at three each night hearing my own voice, asking over and over if it was my fault, if I saw only the Beth I needed to see. I lie awake not because I don't know the answer but because I fear it.

Mary Pollard

Your sister's voice cuts you each morning across your thigh where no one can see. It cuts again at night along your upper arms.

Crawl on your cuts to us. Crawl on voices veined with night. Let us claw inside as if we were you. We shall shine through your blood. All you have to do is open your cuts.

But you don't. You open your hands instead and find them empty. And so you fill them with a razor, a knife, or scissors. You think your husband doesn't know. There is a difference between knowing with the eye and knowing with the heart. He knows with his eye that you stay late after work. But the eye cannot see what you do when you enter the bars the next town over. Last Thursday, a man tied you up to fuck you from behind, and you were sure he would never let you go. You told your husband you went dancing with friends, and he asked no more questions. A wall of stone rises between you. A smaller one rises between you and your daughter, who is almost thirteen—old enough to know with her eyes.

Step off this razor-thin path. Cut away hands that contain nothing but sleep. Time to give up the hands of silence. Time to chart the channels of blood in a new direction. Time to listen to those you dream. To the still voice. The silent voice. The banished voice. A voice shackled by what is unwept. Chained by what is unsaid. A voice that weaves memory on the sharpest of spindles.

Close your eyes and dream of braided hair flying in the night. The swell of ribs between your legs. There is where you belong! Pay the ticket with blood, and we will take you beneath the earth. We are near. Very near.

106

Lecture Five: The Illuminated Buber," Text A
Dr. Frank Baxter, USC

Martin Buber's early twentieth century theological work would hardly seem to relate to current events much less to our understanding of the mole people if it weren't for the fact that a copy of Buber's landmark philosophical treatise, *Ich und Du,* was found about thirty feet down the hole widely believed to be the hole from which M. emerged. Stranger still, the text wasn't discovered until nearly a decade after M.'s appearance, though the hole had been studied extensively in that time. The fact that the book suddenly appeared half buried in the dirt ten years later has been enough for some scientists to dismiss the Buber text entirely, but others, most notably Dr. Weinberg, perhaps the most famous of molopogists, cite the fact that the age of the dirt found within the pages of the text precisely matches the age of the dirt in the surrounding area as strong evidence that the Buber text is authentic.

The critical debate over the veracity of the book has only increased with the recent rash of kidnappings. Some scientists argue that the book had been buried there all along, and that the mole people unearthed it accidentally while digging beneath the neighborhood, while others argue that the mole people purposefully left it there for us to find as an attempt at communication. Any number of theories could account for the book's location in the dirt pile if not for the fact that the book's pages are littered with notes and scribbles in the strange and cryptic language of the mole people.

Though there is some disagreement among linguists regarding the translation of the marginal notes of the

Buber text, the theory put forward by Prof. Weinberg that the marginalia are in fact a response to Buber written in the form of creation myth holds the most weight. Since the finding of "Text A" another illuminated copy of Buber was found in a town twenty miles from the site. The translation of "Text B," as it has come to be known, has proven more difficult, and at this time it remains a cipher. Dr. Weinberg posits that because the mole people seem to communicate through metaphor, and because Buber's work seems to be so clearly important to them (we cite the finding of two separate texts in two separate locations as evidence) it seems logical to assume the stories reflect an attempt by the mole people to establish some sort of "I and Thou" relationship either with Buber himself or with our community of surface dwellers.

What follows is a rough translation of "Text A," as compiled by Prof. Weinberg:

At night in crumbling voices the man and the woman dreamed of Rabbit who in turn dreamed of them. In their dream of the Rabbit's dream there was no sky, and the earth was always being born.

That day was marked by the endless number of unutterable names. Rabbit was determined to sing them all before the world knotted beneath him. And as he sang, the mud kneaded them into being. For three days, the mud people knew they were alive and the darkness was theirs alone, until the fourth day when Worm whispered in Rabbit's ear. *What kind of a world is it without rain?* Rabbit asked Worm why he wanted something that only brought death to his kind, but all Worm said was, *Of course, you cannot have rain without sky."* And so Rabbit breathed out sky.

The rain didn't stop until the tunnels flooded and most of the mud people were washed away. Rabbit searched the tunnels for Worm and found him half-dead in a pool of water. *Why?* he asked, but Worm could only squirm helplessly. *Why?* Rabbit asked again. *I was bored,* Worm replied.

For generations, the mud people accepted Worm's answer until one day a little girl discovered the light that shone through the hole Rabbit had first made in the sky. She stuck her head out and saw that the rain had created a world of light. Because it was so bright, she could not lift her gaze to see the others walking about but instead saw only their shadows on the ground. She tried to step out into this world but found it had no substance, and she sank back into the earth.

She spread word of this other place where the light never stopped shining but where no one had peace because night never came. And the mud people both yearned for this world and felt sorry for its inhabitants, for who could exist without night? So, they decided to sing to them, to sing toward the sky. And deep in the darkest depths of their tunnels they danced, knowing that even if the shadow people could not see or hear them, they would feel their presence and know they were not alone.

Richard Hubbard

I sit on the edge of my bed and stare at the hole in my closet floor. Listen to the voices bubbling forth. *Come! It's easier if you breathe. Sharpen yourself, then drop into the world-hearted deep where light and air ache.* Why don't I move? I am not afraid. And yet I am. Afraid. This is my home. This is my bed. This place, it has a name.

My lids block the path. Why do they not close so that I may find my hour and drop into starless night. Into nowhere. Into a place where if I am asked who I am I will not have a ready answer. Still, my eyes take in traces of a life, an unmistakable life. Years. Years. My gaze groping through years, while paw-fuls of dirt fly forth from the pit, covering my dress shoes, splattering my pants and button-up shirts, spilling into the room.

The phone rings again this morning, but I do not answer. It is the bank wondering why I am not at work. What answer could I possibly give? Should I say I am the one. Not that other. I am the one ticking toward desire. I am the one refusing to sleep. Refusing also to wake. My fingers groping for purchase over my carcass when I am here all along, wide open, waiting to be sewn together.

The doorbell sounds, and again I do not answer. It is my sister checking up on me. What self would I present to her? Should I turn the wheel and see? Am I that one there, standing to the side, smiling through the hour? The one unable to let fugitive hands rest on the man I desire? Or that other. That other I fear to face.

My temple stands, and I sit, staring at a hole in a ruined floor.

Look no more. Come! You are so near to naming your skin. Claw your desire from your chest. Open your mouth to the strong kiss you were meant to receive.

Police Report #6
Detective: Bill Carpenter
Transcribed from the Voice Recorder;
 corner of Hudson and Oak
23, Nov, 2012.

I just finished bagging a dog caught in a mole trap. Not a pretty sight. And it's the second one this week. I don't know what gets into people. I suppose I should be thankful that the roaming mobs are gone. Now they're satisfied with trapping them. They've never seen one, and yet they want to kill them. The way they talk, it's as if the mole people are the only source of evil in the world. I sat behind a group of them in the *Aladdin Diner* at lunch today and you should have heard Norm Pringle going on: "The only problem with poison," he says, "Is you don't get the satisfaction of seeing 'em dead." I'd like to show Norm the dog I found tonight. See what he thinks of that.

They call the males "boars" and the females "sows" as if they were animals. Jim Weaver says he's pretty sure he got a whole "labour" of them by lighting sulfur sticks and stuffing them down the holes. He disagreed with Norm, saying he had the satisfaction of imagining the whole lot of them suffocating and that was a far sight better than seeing just one of them bleeding to death in the jaws of the trap. I almost asked, "What did they ever do to you?" But I didn't. The truth is, someone or something has been doing these kidnappings, and as much as I hate to admit it, the mole people are my only suspects. Still, we have laws in this country. Haven't they heard of innocent until proven guilty? Haven't they heard about the eighth amendment's ban on cruel and unusual punishment? I wonder how they'd like it if someone started pumping gas into the diner.

At least the people of this town have managed a little restraint. There are reports that over in Heath they're wearing the mole people's fur. Personally, I think it's a hoax. Someone's sewn together some raccoon skins or muskrat. But a few people here have heard about it and are talking about starting a furrier company. Why not? they say. We're a capitalist country, and we've got an unlimited supply of product right under our feet, just waiting to be harvested. Harvested! Personally, if anyone in this town starts "harvesting," I'll shut them down so fast their head will spin. The hysteria is bad enough without trying to make money on it.

Only an hour ago, I caught Norm setting a trap inside a hole on the school playground. I thought about asking him if he'd gone insane. Instead, I asked what he was planning on catching on the foursquare court. "I saw one," he told me. "Plain as day. I saw it peeking its head out of this hole."

"Then let's cover up the hole like they seem to be doing with all the others," I said, stepping out of the car with my shovel. "All you're going to do with that trap is hurt yourself or some kid." Norm looked disappointed, as if I'd told him he wasn't invited to my birthday.

Fifteen minutes later, we'd covered the hole back up. I confiscated the trap and a box of sulfur sticks he had in his trunk. Seems he couldn't make up his mind between the steel-jawed trap and the sticks, but in the end decided the trap would still provide the most satisfaction.

Melissa Morton

I wake beneath the earth to darkness and song. Groggy as if recovering from a deep sleep. The syncopated rhythm opens spaces in me. No words I can make out. Only a sort of wail. *When I come to die, I ask of you one favor. That with the braids of your black hair, you tie my hands.* It's a Siguiriya. The oldest of Flamenco songs. I'm sure of it.

A cold hand takes mine. Long fingers wrap about my wrist. The claws pricking my flesh. The wormy breath should be enough to make me run, but instead I step closer. He, or She, or It spins me further into the darkness, then releases me. I take up the hem of my red dress in my hands and stomp my heels to the rhythm. My partner's heels sound in return. Though I see nothing, I know we are dancing, responding each to the other. When he lifts his arms above his head, I dance in a circle around him. When he holds his arms out to me, I move in close. When he waves his hand behind my head, I bend my neck to him, give him my lips, careful never to touch.

There is no more waiting for truth. The song leads us there. It's this half we must deal with. This half we must trust even as the music grows louder, the rhythm chaotic.

I push back the growing fear. The narrow scrapings. The music deafens, quelling my own mouth. And still my partner stomps. Still he calls to me, demanding. He, and I, and us. This fettered threesome caught in the dance. My hands twirl above my head, fingers like twirling birds, calling to him. I can't stop. I don't know how to stop. I don't ever want to stop. What leads us to this place?

All that matters is that you are here. Shiver off your skin. Find new layers beneath the earth. Weave them together in the dance. You are here, tying our hands. You are here, so ask of us one favor.

There are two lines to truth, neither of which I can follow. One line leads down the hole in my bedroom closet, the other leads to him.

The sun drifted in my room today. There can be no more sleep. I would leave this world if I could. If I had the courage, I would follow the line to you my gentle one. My open one. Who says it has to die? Maybe both lines lead to the same world. Maybe the way is down and through. To the dimming place.

Look, I breathe in the cold November air as I walk away. Look at my breath, rising softly, tumbling clouds, a shape of our own making, beloved. But there is no second heaven. If I thought it were possible, I'd follow the line, no matter how dark the way. We came near to living, maybe as near as one can get.

I think that's what the voices want. The voices that rise from the pit beneath my bed. The voices that call to me. The voices I refuse to hear. There is a land called lost, and I intend to end up there. I do not want voices that knead a new me. Some things are better left unsaid. Some deeds better left undone.

Where can I hide from the voices that bloom in my head? I run and run and still they don't recede. Don't they know that speaking to you is worse than voices from the abyss? Worse than darkness and silence and counterfeit homes. I would rather cower before a wall and speak with stone.

And so I run. Each step a letter to one who stood before your door. Each step a stone placed in the mouth of the one who would speak to you. Do not ask to open my words.

We ask with breath.
We ask with wind.
We ask with earth.
We ask with stone.
Remove the moon from your eyes, and the fear will go. Step through to the other side, and there will be no need to close. Speak as you would of fire, and he will warm your hands. There are more than two lines. Follow now, this map that hews words from skin.

Police Report #7
Detective: Bill Carpenter
Unfiled Report
21, Nov, 2012.

*Special Note: This transcription and those that follow were taken from the voice recorder of Detective Bill Carpenter. Officers' O'Malley and Thornton found the recorder in the kitchen of the residence he used to share with his ex-wife, Beth.

I'm tired of waiting. If the brass had their way, we'd all be sitting behind desks, twiddling our thumbs. We don't get many chances like this. In most cases, the holes are blocked or covered over after they're made. The last time a hole was left open was when Mary Pollard disappeared, and even then, it was filled twenty-four hours later. Why wouldn't the higher ups send someone into the tunnels to investigate? They keep saying to wait for the Feds. Some people think it's a conspiracy. I'd say either they're afraid of what's down there, or they're afraid of knowing what's down there. It doesn't make much sense no matter how you cut it. And there's only one way it's going to start making sense.

Flashlight: Check
Rope: Check
Canteen: Check
Fudge Brownie Power Bars: Check
Portable Shovel: Check
Gun: Check

Nothing is going to mess with me down there.

The first fifteen feet or so of descent were damp, but after that it dries out pretty fast. The tunnels are surprisingly comfortable for a human. Don't know what I expected. Mud, I suppose. Low ceilings. I was sure I'd be crawling. I thought there'd be roots and worms hanging from the ceiling, sticking out of the sides, but the walls seem meticulously kept up. If you run your hand along them, they are nearly as smooth as glass.

The first junction's approximately thirty feet in. I took the tunnel to the right. That's my strategy. Keep right. The tunnel seems to be leveling off, too; though if I had to bet, I'd say there's a slight downward grade. I'm moving slow. Listening. Looking for any sign of life. Nothing. I suppose I'm too deep for most burrowing animals. But I should at least see a rat or a prairie dog. I should at least hear water dripping.

The silence is upsetting. It makes my own footsteps seem that much louder. Like I'm stepping on cornflakes. I stop, but it's way too quiet. I turn off my flashlight. That's worse. I'll never do that again. Darkness so thick it smothers you. Darkness like the hand of God over your eyes. I'm pretty sure there's less oxygen down here. I can't say for sure, but I'm definitely breathing harder. Like I'm the one who dug these tunnels.

Another junction. Another right turn. *O you dig, and I dig . . .* Are those voices? I'm pretty sure I'm hearing singing. I'm moving towards it. It's strange. No matter how far or fast I go the voices seem to recede. *And we dig through!* There's been silence going on about a minute now. I put the recorder in my shirt pocket. I think it can still catch my voice. But I need my gun at the ready. I'm not taking any chances.

O one of us. O none of us. O you! The voices are worse than the silence.

I'm not sticking around. The brass was right. Better to leave this alone. Left. Left. I have to get out. Another junction. Take it left. No. Right. No matter which way I turn the voices won't stop. I've got to cover my ears.

Goddamn it! I dropped the flashlight. It's out! The flashlight's out. I'm backed up against a wall. This can't be happening. This darkness. Like ink seeping into my pores. I've got to rub it away. But these aren't my hands. They're connected to my body, at least I think so. But they don't feel like my hands. I rub them together, feel the warmth of the friction. They still aren't my hands. I run my fingers over my face, and it's the same thing. It's not my face. I'm sure of it. I mean, it is my face. I can feel the bump on the ridge of my nose where my brother hit me with a can when I was six. I can even feel the whiskers from my three-day beard. But it's not my face.

I've got to find the flashlight. I'm on my knees, scouring the ground. If I could just shine the light on my hands, then I would know. I could see. Maybe not my face, but I would know.

I've got it! Damn it! It doesn't work! How can it not work? I pound it against the wall. Fuck! My legs. I don't know if my legs are mine any more. I need to run. I've got to get out now, or I'll never leave.

Keep moving. Left. Keep running. The tunnel's going up, I think. It's going up, isn't it? *There is nothing written in your eye we cannot see.* Voices smother me like the darkness. *Nothing etched in your ear we cannot hear. No end to the depths. No end!*

I can't breathe. They're trying to suffocate me. To cut off my air with their voices. Keep going. Just a little farther. My hands are now my eyes. They seek out the contours of the wall, and I follow.

The tunnel opens before me. I've entered a large room. I'm certain of it. The heavy air is gone. The voices have lifted. And I know there is no end.

David Singer

There is a hole in the middle of the embalming room. A hole that calls to me with guttering fingers. See them climb to my ears like roiling vines. Hear the rhymes from the night house. Taste the dirt on their tongues. I will not.

"As practiced in the funeral homes of the Western World, embalming uses several steps. Modern embalming techniques are not the result of a single practitioner, but rather the accumulation of many decades, even centuries, of research, trial and error, and invention."

The skinstripped voices would have me serve them. An orphan to their magnetic master. Lose what I have sowed in the safety of this sepulcher. They would write it away with wandering words. They do not know what a human needs. The less we stand, the better. Better to lie down with the others, to lie down in the light. Lie down on the table and

"Any clothing on the corpse is removed and set aside and any jewelry inventoried. A modesty cloth is sometimes placed over the genitalia. The corpse is washed in disinfectant and germicidal solutions. During this process the embalmer bends, flexes and massages the arms and legs to relieve rigor mortis."

Every I must come to itself. Every I give itself over to voices spun from voids. What is smaller than itself must become larger. Trim hands must open full. Take the ripened fruit never to be forgotten. Step from deathless and into budding.

"The eyes are posed using an eye cap that keeps them shut and in the proper expression. The mouth may be closed via suturing with a needle and ligature."

With heart fingers, I write on the walls of my body.

Yes, we shall bring you home early to suckle. We give you our bodies on which to write. We shall bring you home early to breathe. We give you our untied mouths so you may speak. We shall bring you home early to love. Delight in the sweet brush of words!

Mary Pollard

It's so different from what you think. From the stories people tell. I remember waking to their claws about my head. Long claws that cast shadows. Their teeth like a thousand intact secrets sank into my neck. The poison bloomed in every word. The last thing I saw before sleep was this face like an inverted, pink octopus, looking down at me. I want to know the world that can hold such strange creatures.

And here it is. I wake to the neighing of a horse. Like a lantern in the dark, I follow the sound, seek it out. Round the corner. Down the tunnel. The horse whinnies, and I follow the sound like a stream. No a river whose name I've always known. It is her name. My sister's name. And I say it at last. *Ellen.* It hangs in the air, and now I follow that, too.

Was it a kiss that woke me? Did I mistake the bite for a kiss, the venomed teeth for lips? Sundered from myself, I wake to a new language, woven of desire and despair. I wake with tasteless eyes but a keen mouth able to see a horse in the dark.

I stumble before it, all too aware of the self-inflicted wounds that slice my legs, my arms, marks of all I thought due. I reach out my hand as I draw near, expecting to feel the horse's hot breath on my skin. She bites hard into my uncertain song.

That's when I hear the words of the mole person, sitting in the darkness behind. *Stand for no one. Stand for nothing. For you alone have room.*

She steps closer, nuzzles her head. I'm sure it is a she, though I don't know why. I dare not open my eyes. How often before this I would have fled. Not now. Not this night. This moon is of my own making. I give her my other hand.

When we fear, we feel the tiny itch of desire falling from our throats. When we fear, we wallow through the cry of birds. When we fear, we pinch our fingers to the flame. Do not forget the language of fire!

I'm pretty sure this is the larder where they keep their food. Moles bite the heads off worms before storing them to eat later. I read they can store thousands in their larders. If the same is true for mole people, I don't want to know what's in here.

There are still songs to sing . . . Set your sails earthward . . . Again the voices are all about me . . . Cast *your net north of your past . . . What is called your land is really a mountain! . . .* I'm sure the voices are coming from the heads of the decapitated bodies, heads that lie on the ground around me. I step on something, hear a crack as of bone. I turn to my right and step. Another crack. I turn to my left. The same thing. I can't move. Try as I might, I cannot force my legs to take another step.

I remember the countless times as a boy I tried to escape my life. The time I crawled into the sewer pipe armed only with a few matches. I took off my shoes and rolled up my pants, but I wasn't prepared for the squish and suck of knee-deep mud, the way in which it surrounded your foot. Worse still, I couldn't have foreseen the heightened senses of feet never used to feeling. The way in which a mushy clump under my toes became a decomposed rat, a tickle across my arch a slimy snake. Or the time I walked deep into the spillway beneath the dam. I followed the trickle of water to the great iron door. When I touched it, when I felt the weight of all that water on the other side, I couldn't move. I was so small. I was nothing. And if the doors opened, I would be washed away.

I climb back on the beam of memory. It's all I can do to take the flashlight in my hands once again and shake it. Hoping against hope. The light pierces the dark, scouring the ground for the skulls I'm sure I've stepped on. There are none. Only discarded trinkets among the rocks. Necklaces and earrings shine in the dark. Old shoes and clothes glisten with the dew of silence, shot from the old world to land rejected in the new.

But there is more. I feel its breath before me, graying the black waste. I shine the light ahead of me, and there I am. *I know you. I am in your need.* Did I say that or the figure before me? The figure who is me. Neither of our mouths moved, and yet a voice sounded in my head. I'm sure if I shine the light on my own body, it will no longer be there. I no longer exist. The figure before me is no mirror image. He is wholly real. It is I who feel flat, false in comparison. Or better, as if I am wholly mad.

He reaches out his hand.

Richard Hubbard

They are done with their digging, so why do they not come for me? Why do they leave me here? Better to be kidnapped. Bitten. Paralyzed. Taken away in the night. I sit on my bed, staring at the dark hole. The hole stares back at me, black, like memory's wound.

Look. There I am a teenager wrestling with Tom. Do you see how he pins me with desire? Do you see how I let myself be pinned, my gaze grubbing toward him?

Look again. John, my best friend in college invites me to his dorm. After a few beers, we loosen up and sit side-by-side watching *Superman.* He admits it's his favorite movie, and I laugh because it's mine, too. Do you see how his hand brushes against my own after the shared laughter? Do you see how my hand pulls away?

Look. It's Thanksgiving at my sister's, and I am the only one without a partner. "When are you going to get married?" my mother asks as she passes the mashed potatoes. I smile politely and say, "I haven't found the right person yet," but my gut churns with the truth that I will never find the right person. The truth I cannot name.

Look at this half death.

Once upon a time, there was a boy   And they lived happily ever after, forevermore. The story lies in the hole between.

Through that hole you must travel. Out of memory and into . . .

Where? Where can I go where I will not gasp for air? Where can I hide that the brackish boy will not find me? Deep in the hole there is a brightness as of voices crumbling toward the sea's reflection. I will not listen.

I cannot keep up this blind-dream. I am a castaway cleansing the world with my steps. The music plays. My partner claps, stomps his feet, and I sing words I didn't know existed: *I curse my fate. I curse you, as I curse the hour in which I knew you.*

Here I must live myself through without time. But I'm not sure I'm fit. Not sure I'm up to this dance. My partner commands me, and I lift my feet. I twirl round and round singing words I'm only beginning to understand: *I don't know without you, without you, with no Thou.*

I spin closer to my partner, laying my hands on his shoulders. Why can I not see him? I must know who drives me to these immortal heights, whom I hold while everything slips away. But the closer I get, the darker the air about me, until it's like ink washing over me.

I slap him. We sway apart, then back together again.

I shake him. We tumble down moon-swept dunes into the odor of dance.

The music builds, tossing us together. I wait for the crescendo, for the shard of rhythm that binds. I take his head in my hands and kiss him.

I know every scar those lips have suffered. I have felt the shape of their loneliness in bed at night. My partner is no man. No stranger.

My own hand has held this piece of home.

My own feet have led me through this tumult.

Wake! she whispers into my mouth. Or I into hers.

This thing I cannot name rises within, carrying us across the weeping.

Police Report #9
Detective: Bill Carpenter
Report continued from November 21, 2012:

His grip is firm, the extra thumb holding tight about my wrist. He reaches for my flashlight with his other hand. I'm sure he is going to take it, but he simply turns it off. We wander through darkness. The larder is much bigger when you trust to touch.

Moans sound from every side. *Brother who fell from earth, stay away.* Yet another cries: *Stay awhile, brother.* I walk through the discordant voices as if through waves. I don't know why I let him take me. I'm not easily led. And yet I follow closely, matching his steps. The more we walk, the darker it seems to get, though how it could get any darker I cannot say. Already it is as if the night crawls on my skin.

I do not falter even as the air grows thick about me, and I know the walls are narrowing. We must be in some sort of alcove or antechamber. I remember scuba diving one hundred feet below the surface, feeling the weight of all that water. The pressure was overwhelming. It feels like that now. My guide stops just before I ask where we're going. *It is here for us,* he says.

"Here what?" I answer, though even as I ask, I fear I know the answer. I don't want to be here. Not with her. Not now. I am not ready for this.

He releases my hand, and I fight the urge to run.

She steps forward from the darkness. Beth. It is Beth. I have traveled God knows how far beneath the earth to face my ex-wife. It must be some kind of joke.

We are beginning, my guide says, my guide who is

me. And yet not me. I don't know how I understand him. He speaks so strangely, as if his voice was carried on many tongues.

"Beginning what?" I ask, and that's when he grasps my shoulders and pulls me close. I can taste the wormy earth on his breath.

In the undivided, there is a binding light," he whispers, bringing his mouth to my neck. I can't see it, but I feel that pink nose tickle my skin, and I'm not about to wait for the tiny, razor teeth, and the paralyzing poison.

"I don't know what your game is," I tell him, though I'm looking past him at her. "But I'm not playing. I'm not doing this."

He steps back into the darkness, leaving me to face her.

"You left me," I say, quietly. "You walked out."

"You didn't give me a choice." She steps closer as if she would burrow inside me.

"*I* didn't give you a choice!" My lips and tongue swell with the blackness. My chest tightens like a tourniquet, one that won't let anything in. "What choice did *you* give me? You left me alone."

"We were already alone. You didn't want anything else." She reaches out her hand to me. Her fingers grace my cheek.

I step away. I don't know why because part of me wants to take her in my arms. To take her and walk deeper into the darkness. But I step away, and when I do, she hesitates.

Then the thing that is me steps into my beam of light.

You cannot fight the song in your head, he says. *There is a hole that will not go away.*

"Shut up!" I yell. "I still have a chance."

You don't want the chance. You want the hole. The hole that suffocates. The hole that itches.

"Fucker!" I step closer and raise the flashlight above me. "You lying fuck!"

How your face reddens after I bite. You'll do anything to keep that hole open, except to step inside.

"I did step inside! I walked right in and kept on walking!"

Did you?

I hit him in the head, and he falls to the ground with a thud.

She and I stand alone, each facing the other as possibility bleeds out.

"You can't make me do this," I say, as I kick him with my boot. "It's my story."

Then I'm off and running down one of the tunnels. I don't know if it's the one I came in, but I don't care. I don't know if she's following me. I don't know if I'm afraid she will or afraid she won't. I just keep on running. And after I run far enough, I'm no longer sure what they were trying to do. Maybe she wanted to trap me here, to make me her slave in some kind of sick perversion of the surface world. Maybe he wanted to change places with me, to lock me up in his larder and live my life.

I hit a wall hard. Bloodied my nose. It's better if I go slower, feel my way along the walls. First junction right. Second junction left. I'm pretty sure I'm going up. I have to be. There is no song. No voices anymore.

Another right. Left. Or was it a left, then right. I'm not sure. I don't know if the darkness is getting to me or if I gave myself a concussion back there, but I can't think straight. I'm feeling a bit faint. But I've got to keep moving. That's all I can do. I still have a few hours worth of batteries in my flashlight. And I've got my PowerBars. I'll be okay. I know what I'm doing. I don't want this. I know that. I want my old life. The one with her before she left. No! Not that one. I want the one after. The one where I knew who I was. Where I thought I knew. What I would give to be sitting in our house once again, sipping my wine with her beside me, staring out at the night sky, knowing no other shore.

Annie Clarkson

I lie beneath my desk at the staffing company, the only place free of desire. I will not darken to you. Yet you come, flayed from the depths. I watch as your claws pierce through the commercial-grade carpet. I wait with wondrous wounds as pawful after pawful of dirt piles beside the pit. Why do you do this to me? Why can I not simply move on? Instead, I lie here, grounded by nothingness, free to fly with you into the longest listening. I hear you already, asking that I choose you in place of all the rest. Asking that I drink from your mouth, when I fear it is filled with dirt.

But when you surface from the pit you say nothing. Ask nothing of me. As if the decision is entirely mine. The choice echoes in my head, calling to memory: The time you fed me ice cream from your spoon. The time you did that impression of the Brooklyn cop and made me laugh so hard I peed my pants. The time I could not say goodbye to you, knowing it might be the last. Neither of us able to speak.

Before I could at least pretend. I could dream of leaving and call it a choice. But now you stare at me with black eyes, sitting at the edge of your hole, asking me to climb out of myself.

This place should not be named. Ever. This place where I will be haunted by memory no matter which choice I make. This place they call life, when it is nothing but a stuttering. In which I am nothing but a name dripping beneath a desk.

Still, the dark eyes demand when all I can do is murmur. Lick my wound open. Lick the blade wide across the wrist. The only answer I have the strength to give.

134

David Singer

I stand above you,
lapping home.
No sentence pins me
to this death-sized box.

I stand before you,
in fevered grass,
falling through settled floors
to rest in a hidden corner.

I stand beside you,
waiting for the ocean's song,
drinking the flaked gold
from the sparks of my new name.

I didn't know I was coming,
didn't know the night
would lay claim
to such a large sky.

I crawl across this
lonely map to hear
all in your mouth. I
climb down the sleepless walls

of earth and stand in
you to say this
as if we can be
other than fire.

Police Report #10
Detective: Bill Carpenter
Report continued from November 21, 2012:

Midnight. I've come full circle. Back to the house Beth and I lived in. Back to the house in which she left me. It's been eight months. Two months since I moved out, looking to escape. And now I'm back. I could've run. When I emerged from the tunnel outside Skyline Park, I could have gotten in my car and just kept on driving. Maybe I should have, but I had to come here.

It's breaking and entering. I know that. The couple that bought the place lies soundly asleep upstairs. But I just had to see it again. Something in me has shifted, and I don't know who I am. Maybe I'm hoping the house will tell me. Maybe I'm wondering if it's my life that's shifted and not me.

If you've never walked through a home that once contained your life, a home now occupied by the life of someone else, I don't recommend it. I'd particularly caution against doing it at night. I don't know how a house can absorb memories. They take them into their walls like smoke. Well, this place reeks of memories. You see a picture on a wall in the exact place you'd hung the photo of you and your wife standing at a bar, arms around each other and laughing on your first anniversary. But it's not a picture of you and your wife. It's a picture of someone's father as a young man in the army. You see the dent in the doorway of the living room you made when you and your wife carried in the couch the day you moved in. Only, the brown leather sofa has been replaced by a green chenille love seat. The past was merely a dream.

The present is no different.

It was a mistake to come here. It's better to move on and not look back. No one should have to wander through the altered landscape of their past. But there's a noise in the kitchen. Some sort of scratching.

She emerges from the hole in the middle of the linoleum floor, dirt piled all around. It's Beth, though you could also say it's not Beth, what with that strange pink nose, like an inverted octopus. And those oversized forepaws and razor sharp claws. It's Beth. I can tell by the way my breath catches when I see her. The way my chest caves in, as if I've been hit with a two by four. The body knows even when the mind plays its tricks.

Why did she follow me? Who am I kidding? I knew she'd follow, and I knew I wanted it.

She steps toward me, reaching out her hand the way she did in the burrow.

"I don't want your love any more. I don't need it."

She doesn't say a word. Not a goddamn word. Just takes another step toward me. Both arms out now.

"I'm past it, damn it! Past you!"

Another step forward.

"Who do you think you are?" I ask. "You think you can just come back like this and everything will be the same?"

Another step.

"Everything is NOT the same," I shout. I don't care if I wake the owners. "I'm not the same!"

She takes another step so that she stands directly before me.

"It's like I live two lives now," I say. "The old one keeps coming back, telling me how things could have

137

been. I can't even call what I do now a life. I spend most of the day shoveling away memories. Stomping them deep down so they won't come back to the surface again. But they keep coming. They keep coming!"

She reaches her hand toward my face.

"Don't touch me!" I shout, swatting her hand away.

She steps back, and the scent of her fear releases something in me. Something I'd wanted to let out for a long time.

"Get the hell away from me!" I shout as I bore down on her.

I hit her, and she cowers like a dog.

"Go back to wherever you came from!" I say. "I don't want you any more." I hit her again, as she uses her hands to shield her head.

She crawls back toward the hole.

"That's it, leave me again," I say. And she does. She disappears down the hole. I fight for control of my breath, but it flaps like a wrecked sail in my mouth. I know what I have to do.

I run back to my car and pull Norm's box of sulfur sticks from the trunk. One by one, I light them and drop them down the hole in the kitchen. When I'm done, I shovel the dirt back in.

Norm Pringle was wrong. There is no satisfaction in gassing. Without a body, there is nothing to stop the past from flooding your world. And now I have one more memory to add: The picture of her face, hands raised to shield it from my blows.

138

Mary Pollard

I am the story of a woman who cuts. I dream my story as I sleep between worlds. Now I have dug back the dark hours. I have set loose the knives behind my eyes. All because of this horse who nuzzles. A horse I cannot see, but feel as I would the hydrangeas in my house.

Let us leap shadows, you and I, a voice behind me whispers. At first I think it is my sister's voice, but then I know it's my own. Or rather not quite my own. *Know not too carefully,* the voice says. I don't speak like that. At least I didn't.

The creature takes my hand and places it on the horse's neck. The next thing I know I'm on the horse. I'm sitting on the horse in a darkness so thick I can taste it. *Don't leave a bite, of earth,* the voice says. There is a loud slap against the horse's behind, and I'm off, running.

I cling tight as we canter through the cavern. If I wasn't so scared, I would take the knife from my pocket and cut deep. I would cut over and over again. But I cannot let go. The sound of hooves like thunder. If I sit up, I will bash my head on a rock. I'm sure of it. The darkness dizzies, so I squeeze shut my eyes and wait for it to end. But it doesn't end.

I am alone on the horse, running through the dark where no stars glitter.

I am alone. On a horse.

Nothing between us. Nothing around us.

In sight of nothing I break open to you gentle one.

In spite of night, I let go, spread my arms like wings, and bloom.

Epilogue:

In response to recent progress interpreting the language and mythos of the mole people, Dr. Xander of the Berkeley Psychiatric Institute has put forward a theory that has slowly gained many adherents. In his paper entitled, "The Mole People: Saviors or Delusion," he argues quite convincingly that the mole people don't exist at all. The cornerstone of his argument centers on the "evidence" or lack thereof. He points out the obvious, that "The Illuminated Buber Texts" are written with a blue, Bic ballpoint, for ex. In laboratory tests, Dr. Xander has shown that traditional moles are unable to grasp a ballpoint in their paws, though a significant number were able to hold a pencil. While Dr. Xander never deals with the fact that the mole people may quite possibly have evolved differently to traditional moles, there are those in the scientific community who see his experiment as a blow to the authenticity of the A and B texts. Further, the recent scandal involving Drs Brady, Prilutsky, Gu, and Roy has cast a pall over their report of the capture of the only known mole person, M. The fact that they falsified findings in their earlier study of mammalian neurotoxins has in the eyes of many discredited all of their subsequent research.

Dr. Xander painstakingly points out that the recent frenzy over the mole people likely has more in common with the occasional periods of religious hysteria in our history than with actual encounters with an as yet undiscovered species. Further, it is his assertion that our infatuation with the mole people simply represents the rise of a new religion or cult, more specifically, that the hysteria surrounding this new cult is merely a reflection of contemporary society's need to believe in something other when science has stripped away any and all hope in more traditional manifestations of that other. He cites the growing number of temples to the mole people as clearly significant, but goes on to mention as further evidence the graffiti spray painted on walls, saying "M. lives!" and the numerous books popping up in the New Age section of bookstores with titles like *Getting in Touch with Your Inner Mole Person* or *The Six Agreements: One for each Mole Finger.*

Dr. Xander provides a convincing case, and he has attracted much attention of late. However, if one thing is clear in the nascent study of the mole people, it is that scientific opinion has changed course numerous times. In short, the jury is still out. All we can say after a decade of scouring the literature is that there is no clear evidence either way. The only thing that seems clear is that we need them. We need the mole people as they need us. We strain to hear them even as we cover our heads with pillows to drown them out: *Are you afraid to walk through a night both light and dark? Hold fast my hand and let your shadow go.* Science may seem to give us rational answers. Literature and philosophy may seek to give us a framework so that we can pretend to understand. Religion may offer us a way of seeing ourselves. All these things may even give us comfort for a time. But they are not enough. Not nearly enough. Then the voices call to us again. Voices that drill through rock. Voices that crawl across our bedroom floors. Voices that lie between us as we sleep. Their words arrive glistening with earth, daring us to dig our own holes, suffocating us until we open our eyes only to see our own faces in this strange story.

Photo by Gary Isaacs

PETER GRANDBOIS is the author of the novel *The Gravedigger*, selected by Barnes and Noble for its "Discover Great New Writers" program, *The Arsenic Lobster: A Hybrid Memoir*, chosen as one of the top five memoirs of 2009 by the Sacramento News and Review, *Nahoonkara*, winner of the gold medal in literary fiction in *ForeWord* magazine's Book of the Year Awards for 2011, and a collection of surreal flash fictions, *Domestic Disturbances*. His essays, plays, and short stories have appeared in numerous journals and been shortlisted for both the Pushcart Prize and Best American Essays. He is an associate editor at *Boulevard* magazine and teaches at Denison University in Ohio.